Prison is not the usual place to discover love, forgiveness and the grace of God. But that's where Hunter Lowe finds it. *Because He Cares, Revised*, is the story of Hunter's spiritual battle as God works in his life before, during, and after five years in prison.

Walk with Hunter through his idyllic high school years, into a modeling career with hopes for acting. **Fall** with him into a moral defeat that takes him to prison. **Stand** with Hunter as he travels through his darkest hours including a vicious beating that ends any career that depends on good looks. **Watch** how he recovers into a new life with the help of family and friends, a new cellmate and an NFL player. **Share** the victories of Hunter's soul from prison to being happily married and a respected person in his community.

Because He Cares, Revised, comes out of one of America's serious contemporary issues through suspense, a touch of violence, romance, forgiveness, failures, and victories. Hunter's journey to Christ is the same we all must take, in prison or not.

Because He Cares

Roy Swanberg

Sterling Rock
Books

BECAUSE HE CARES

Copyright © Roy Swanberg 2015

ISBN: 978-1508675075

Revised from the original book first published in America
by Lighthouse Christian Publishing in 2007

*This book is a work of fiction. Names, places, characters
and incidents are the product of the author's imagination.
Any resemblance to actual events or places or persons,
living or dead, is entirely coincidental.*

Bible quotations from the New International Version (NIV)
Copyright © 1973, 1978, 1984 by International Bible Society

Published by
Sterling Rock Books
576 Boyd Ave.
Princeton
IL 61356
United States of America

Other books by Roy Swanberg:

Book One: *Jason's Promise, No Choice, No Option, No Other Way.* Jason discovers some situations in life just cannot be changed.

Book Two: *Jason's Promise, Put to the Test.*
Jason meets the moral and ethical challenges of college life and law school.

Book Three: *Jason's Promise, Fulfilled.*
The story of Jason in the roughness of the political arena.

Chapter One

"Hunter Thomas Lowe! Just what *is* your problem?" Yes, my grossly overweight, seething director, C.J. was yelling at me again. "You're in this modeling agency because of your good looks and great body, but now you're just a klutz. You've just fallen off a twenty thousand dollar motorcycle and almost destroyed it."

Trying to lift it back up, I said, "Sorry, C.J., I just…"

He swore in a voice that could have stripped wallpaper off walls three blocks away. With red blood vessels bulging out all over his face and bad breath swirling in the three inches of space between us, he yelled like an angry baseball manager to an umpire.

"Don't give me this 'sorry' stuff, Lowe. It's been a long hard week for all of us. We've had enough stress today to kill each other." Turning to all the others in the studio, he continued his rant while stomping around and throwing papers all over the set. "Nothing's getting done here today. You might as well all leave. Get out of my sight, all of ya — photographers, makeup, and the whole lousy mob. Have a good week-end — I sure won't."

In the sudden silence that followed that display of

1

raw nerves, the hot lights, motorized clicking cameras, and dozens of retakes quickly came to an end. Without another word, Bart and Jerry, the two models I was working with, and I never looked back. We changed out of the biker clothes we were wearing, left the building, ran to our sports cars, and raced three blocks to *Tommy's Tap*.

It was Friday night and we usually got there for happy hour to unwind, and were earlier than normal this night. I was the first one through the old dusty screen door. "Tommy, I'll have my usual — a Coke."

That's all Bart and Jerry needed. They came at me like a cheating wrestling tag team. Bart started in on me first.

"Lowe! Just what are you trying to prove to the world with this Coke bit?"

"What do you mean?"

"Gimme a break. For about a year now you've come into this bar a couple times a week, and only ordered a Coke or a 7UP." Swinging his arms like a tour director, then slapping the shiny bar three times, he went on. "This is as bar, Lowe. A bar! People drink in here. Don't you get it?"

Thumping his finger deep into my chest and pushing me back a few steps, Jerry said, "Yeah, in a perfect world you'd be smart, but like he just told you, this here's a *bar*. People drink beer in this joint! What don't you understand about that?"

I grinned the best I could. "I come in here to hang out with you guys. You know I don't drink. I didn't think that was a problem with ya."

"You afraid of, getting messed up like us? Hey, have you ever had a beer, Lowe?" Bart said.

"A few times in high school, good sense told me to drop it like a bad habit."

I never did like walking into the dark and smelly *Tommy's Tap*. It was just an old derelict house with crumbling and torn 1958 phony yellow brick tarpaper siding. It survived bravely on the west edge of town by the mainline Santa Fe railroad tracks. Ten years ago Tommy Fisher resuscitated the dying farmhouse by converting it into a dingy tavern mainly by just painting over the windows. Tommy himself was a reflection of the dump. He only shaved every few days, and always wore a dirty rubber apron that struggled to contain his protruding girth, testifying to the generous consumption of his own beer.

Every time a fast freight rolled by, less than fifty feet away, I had to cover my glass to protect it from dust sifting down from the rafters. The only real lights in the place were a couple of dim neon, beer-advertising displays hanging in the paint smeared windows. I could never understand how a guy could make a pigsty like this into a business, much less show a profit.

The foggy blue air from poorly hidden cigarettes under the bar swirling around even tasted like beer when I took a breath. Secondhand smoke and secondhand beer. This was a hovel the E.P.A. really should have closed down. But it was the only place I could hang out with these guys, other than at work. They weren't such a bad bunch, but they sure hounded me on this drinking issue. That night they kept up the pressure.

"We're going to wear you down some night, Lowe." Bart started in again, "and we're gonna knock that halo off your good-looking head, too."

"Not in this lifetime." *I wish these jerks would stop pushing me.*

"The kind of work we do grinds us down. Ya gotta learn to relax and live, deacon. You're missing all the fun."

"Yeah, well I'll risk it. I'm staying with the soft stuff. Anyway, what do you mean, 'deacon'?"

"Well, that soft stuff as you call it ain't as good for you as this here beer. You some kind of religious nut?"

"Of course not. Do I look like one?"

"Hunter Lowe, the religious freak. Have you ever been drunk? You're twenty-three. You must have been drunk sometime."

That's a hard question for a twenty-three-year-old guy to answer in a place like this, but I'm not going to start lying my way through life now. "Never. So what does that prove?"

"Twenty-three years old and never been wasted? Sheee, Lowe, wish I could say that. But it don't fly in the real world. A couple beers don't hurt nobody."

I shook my head. "You guys have been shoveling me that pile for a year now. Give it a rest." Spinning around on the bar stool, sipping the Coke, I went on, "You look like you're having fun, but when I see how you act after you sop up the stuff, I hope I never drink."

Jerry snickered. "Ya know, you're too moral for your own good. A crack like that could bust up a good friendship – but I'll let slide this time, Lowe"

"Get off your high horse," Bart added. "Like I said, a beer or two never hurt nobody. I'll even buy the first one, I'll even –"

"And I'll buy the second one." Jerry said.

Farther down the bar, Tommy whispered out of the side of his mouth, so others wouldn't hear, "After listening to this dim-witted argument for a year, I'll buy the third. Bottoms up, kid."

"There ya go, Lowe, three free beers. Wish someone would offer me a deal like that!"

A shiver shot up my spine. Something snapped in my head. After a year of arguing I banged my fist on the bar and threw these so called friends a look of defeat mixed with anger and fear. I finally said, "Look, if I have a stupid beer, will you guys shut up and get off my case?"

"Yes! We broke him like a horse," Jerry yelled as he raised a fist high in victory. "Hey, Tommy, give our friend here a beer."

"That's three free beers, Lowe!" Bart yelled. "This is your lucky night."

Tommy grinned, shook his head and snatched a glass off the overhead rack. He reached for the closest long tap handle, poured a beer down the inside of the glass and slid it down the bar to me leaving a trail of foam behind it. "Bottoms up, kid."

Chapter Two

Bottoms up, bottoms up, I said to myself. *After all these years I don't believe I'm actually doing this. I hope Gwen and the guys back in Ravenswood never hear about it.*

When I took the first sip, my two friends and Tommy laughed and high-fived each other over their conquest. It was just as bitter as I remember the sip or two of beer I had in high school, but as much as I disliked it, I drained the glass. Bart was the first to speak, of course.

"See, Lowe, the world's still here, still spinning. Nothing's changed."

"I haven't changed my mind," I said slowly. "I still don't like it, and I don't see what the big deal is in drinking beer."

Over the next few hours the subjects of the conversations changed as others joined or left the group. Jerry and Tommy made good on their promises to buy me the next two rounds. The second beer was easier to drink, and the third easier yet. Knowing a bit about barroom etiquette myself, I forced myself to buy each of them a round or two. Can't remember how many.

When the red clock on the wall with little bubbles running around it turned to a blurry 2:00 AM, I knew I had enough of this sorry evening. I also knew I lost the battle. I felt defeated and ashamed with myself.

"Izzz getting late," my swollen tongue mumbled. "I've done enough damage to myself tonight. I hope you guyz are happy now, I'm goi..."

"Good going, Lowe. Now we know you're as low as we are, congratulations."

Congratulations for getting drunk? I never thought it would happen to me. I feel terrible.

I saw Bart and Jerry smile, wink at each other and exchange low-fives under the bar.

"Yeah, yeah, I'm real proud of myzelf. You guyz go on drinking. I'm tired and I gonna leave. You guyz got me drunk just like you wanted to for a long time." I had to catch myself as I almost slid off the stool. My first few steps were clumsy.

"Better wait a few minutes before you leave," Jerry said. "Have some coffee."

"Oh yeah, coffee to make me a wide awake drunk instead a just a tired one, right? Whatz with you guys? You always been telling me a couple a beers don't hurt nobody. Lez zee."

Bart came back with, "You had five or more. That was too much to start with."

"A coupla beers don't hurt," I said again sarcastically, with as much venom as I could. "A coupla beers don't hurt nobody." I couldn't clear my mind of that excuse. "I'm outta here."

"Hey, kid, you sure you okay?" Tommy yelled from the other end of the bar.

"Yeah, I only had five or som'pn, I donno, some friendz you are. You zure mezzed me up tonight." In anger and shame I kicked the old door open and slammed it shut after me, knowing the dust would roll back into the bar.

The cool fresh night air outside made me feel better when I left that hole, but I stumbled a few times on a crack or two in the crummy sidewalk on the way to my car. It took three tries to punch the remote opener in the right place to unlock the door, but once inside, by habit, I got the key into the ignition without any trouble.

I started the engine, pulled away from the curb, and was halfway to the corner when I realized I never even looked back when I pulled away from the curb. *Just dumb luck* I thought. I also noticed my seatbelt wasn't on. As I fumbled for it, I could see all the colored lights and signs looked blurry, wrinkling and weaving back and forth.

Without paying attention to my driving I finally got the belt fastened. When the heat in the car began to rise, even my thoughts turned fuzzy.

I had a cupla beers...
I'll never tell Gwen...
Never shudda given into them guys...
I don't think I oughta done that...
This has got to be a bad dream ..
Maybe I should stop and get some sleep...
I had no business going into Tommy's Tap...

All the lights look red…

But some stand still and some keep moving…

As the thoughts piled up, my head began to hurt. I kept blinking and opening my eyes wide. Shaking my head back and forth I tried to clear my brain. I opened the window and stuck my head out like a dog. *Like a dog? I've become like a dog?* I gripped the steering wheel tight because I felt I was falling.

More blurry lights, then a large beige blob moved in front of me. *The brake, the brake. Where's the brake?* I heard screeching tires, a woman's scream, a loud and heavy thud, sounds of twisting, bending, ripping steel, breaking glass. The air bag hit my chest like a line drive from home plate and took my breath away. The greasy powder sprayed from the bag and I felt liquid and shards of glass all over me. In a long instant and a blinding white flash, something told me my whole life would never be the same again.

Chapter Three

I didn't remember a thing right after the crash, until voices drifted out of my groggy darkness from far off. I was still behind the wheel of my car in a mess of dust, glass, and grease. I began to make out twirling and pulsating white, red, and blue lights, the noise of heavy diesel engines running, and voices crackling on radios. I was in the center of a serious accident. The voices of men were talking of getting doors open, children out and even whispers of a woman who seemed to be dead in the wreckage. My thoughts flashed to my girlfriend, Gwen. I felt relieved when I realized she wasn't with me. Yet some woman died?

Large, strong arms tried to pull me out of the car, and I heard a firefighter yell to a police officer nearby, "I think you'd better come here. This kid's been drinking."

He's not talking about me. I don't drink. So who else is in my car?

Finally a bunch of muscle got me out of the twisted metal, but when I stood up, my legs gave way and I started to slide on the mix of oil and water in the street. A police officer grabbed me to keep me from falling, but I twisted angrily away from him, and yelled, "Keep your hands off me."

He stumbled backwards as I pushed him, tripping over a fire hose, and landing flat on his back in the wet street on broken glass. Some officers jumped to his aid and another bunch of police swarmed onto me, throwing me to the pavement. I felt an awful pain in my back where someone's knee was pushing down, and others stretching my arms behind me were not being any too careful. For the first time in my life I was in handcuffs. They hauled me up and slammed me into a police car, banging my head on the doorjamb. In my stupor, I felt like an animal being shoved into a cage.

My mind was reeling out of control. I couldn't stand anyone touching me or even telling me what to do. With my hands cuffed behind me, I flayed and twisted my body as much as I could. Quickly they shackled my feet to anchors on the floor of the car. They tried to ask me questions, but I spit back answers that made no sense, not even to me. In all this turmoil I felt I was watching one of those police TV shows. My actions and words seemed to be coming from someone else.

In his anger, the officer I pushed yelled, "Get him out of my sight!"

Same words C.J. yelled at me at work a few hours before.

As they were getting the car ready to go, I demanded, "What happened? Why am I here?"

"What's your name, kid?" one of the officers asked.

"Hunter. Hunter Lowe."

"You don't know what you've done?"

"No, no I don't," I yelled back. "Just what did I do?"

"Calm down," one of the officers said. "You'll know soon enough."

"Don't tell the creep," the other cop in the front seat said. "Let him find out when he wakes up tomorrow. Read him his rights."

"You're under arrest. Anything you say . . ."

The officer put the car into gear and we sped away. I don't know how long the drive took to the county jail because I blacked out a few times. What was my pride and joy of a new sports car a minute ago was not even on my mind. I never saw it after that night. When we got to the jail they dragged me to a holding cell and dumped me like a sack of grain on a gray vinyl mat lying on a three inch high slab of concrete. All my ears picked up was something about, ". . . in the morning."

Three hundred miles upstate, on the campus of Northwestern Illinois Christian College (N.I.C.C.,) a red digital alarm clock flashed to 4:43 AM. It was on the desk next to my sleeping girlfriend, Gwen Martin. Of course, I didn't know this at the time. To tell the truth, I didn't know anything at the time – not even where *I* was. She told me all this later.

She said she was in deep sleep, dreaming that she was with her mom and dad in their family room back home in Ravenswood. In her dream they were talking about me, and the ever-growing topic of Gwen and me getting married. It was just a matter of time.

In Gwen's hazy dream that night she was talking with her parents, and waiting for my usual Friday night call. Muffin the dog began to twitch, growl, and bark angrily. The unusual outburst surprised Gwen and her parents, coming from the calm and happy Muffin. When the phone started to ring in her dream, Gwen said she could feel her heart jump with the same excitement it did whenever I walked into a room where she was with her friends.

"*My Hunter!*" Her arms wanted to jump into the phone and hold me, but she couldn't move. Her hands were paralyzed as the phone rang and rang. She looked at the noisy phone and then at her folks, but she just couldn't answer it.

"Help me!" she called out to her parents. "Answer it for me."

Her folks just looked at each other. Suddenly they began to cry, and then quickly left the room. The phone kept ringing while Gwen remained frozen on the couch helpless to move, listening to the ringing, ringing, ringing.

Like the popping of a balloon, Gwen found herself awake and fighting knotted sheets and blankets in her dorm room as she tried to reach for her cell phone still ringing. Megan, her roommate sounded angry. "Answer your dumb phone or turn it off."

"Yeah, yeah, what time is it anyway?"

"Gwen, the phone."

"Four forty-three in the morning! Who? Must be Hunter."

She told me how she fumbled with the little phone and even dropped it on the carpet as she tried to get it to stop ringing. "Hello, Hunter? Hunter? Who?"

"No, this isn't Hunter. It's me, Bruce Cunningham. Hunter's friend from high school. You know me."

I can imagine how surprised she was to hear another voice at that hour, when she was expecting mine. "Why are *you* calling me at this time?"

"Gwen, I'm sorry to call you like this. Is Megan with you?"

"Sure, Megan's here. Why?"

By now Megan was wide-awake in her own bed on the other side of the room knowing something bad was up. She turned on the lamp while Gwen pressed the phone tighter to her ear.

Gwen told me she nearly threw the phone down in panic. "Hunter? Is it something about Hunter? Bruce, tell me, tell me now. Is Hunter okay?"

"I'm sure he's okay, but he's been in a real bad car accident in Capital City. His dad says he's okay, but Gwen …" Bruce paused and Gwen heard him swallow hard and even sniffle. "Gwen, he's in jail. He drove his car into a van, killed a woman, and he was drunk."

"Stop it! That's mean. Stop talking like that! You know as well as I do Hunter doesn't drink at all. Bruce, what's with you?"

Gwen said she could hear Bruce's voice breaking up. "Hunter's dad just called me and told me. I don't know anything more. He's going to Capital City tomorrow to get the details. Gwen, I'm so sorry. I wish I could help you."

Gwen told me all this later and she said she made her mind up instantly. "I'm going to Capital City now!"

"Gwen, no, please don't. You know Aaron and I would take you there ourselves right now — if it would do any good. Let's wait until Hunter's dad finds out what's up. Maybe this is all a mistake."

"Bruce, I want to go to him. I really do."

"I know you do. So do I, but it's best you pray for now. You do that well. I'm sorry I called you at this hour, but I knew you'd want me to."

"Bruce, I don't care where I am or what time it is. Call me anytime. Call me the instant you hear something. Professors don't want us to have our cell phones on, but I will. Please call?"

"Sure, Gwen, we love you."

Reluctantly Gwen swiped her phone off, wanting to hold on to Bruce for assurance. She turned to Megan, who must have guessed something bad had happened. Gwen said that they embraced and started to pray.

Chapter Four

Daylight snuck into the cell through the small window high on the wall, but my nightmare continued. A boot at the end of a guard's leg woke me up. "Hey, kid, wake up. You're special day is here."

Looking around I suddenly realized I was in a jail. "Hey, this is a jail. Where's my belt? I don't belong here, I'm leaving." I only took two long strides towards the door when a guard grabbed my arm and said, "Kid, you *do* belong here. Never mind where your belt is."

"Huh? Where's the bathroom? I have to go to the bathroom."

"Boy, you *are* new here. It's right over there in the corner. Don't you see it? Hurry up. A State's Attorney is here to see you. We'll have to wait till after you talk to him to book you and clean you up."

In the first hangover of my life, I still didn't have control of my attitude or my mouth. "Why do I need to see a State's Attorney? What's a State's Attorney?"

"You'll find out all about it," the guard said, "He's here to charge you with reckless homicide, and to set a time for your first appearance."

"Appearance for what?" I spit back.

"To see a judge. What you really need now, kid, is a lawyer."

"Why?"

"I'm sure he'll tell you why. Now clean up."

The guard had the same hard attitude I remembered from the police the night before. While I was washing my face, the cool water brought back some of my better manners. I began to realize where I was and could feel the confining of the cell. The way they were treating me was a new experience. An experience of falling into an unknown bottomless pit. Not knowing what to grab hold of.

At the door a man dressed in a suit introduced himself as Mr. DeSalvo, State's Attorney. He acted surprised when I stuck out my hand to greet him. He looked just like the lawyers on TV — suit and tie, shined shoes, and a briefcase. I was wearing the dirty, wet, and torn clothes I was brought in with. Used to being well dressed and clean, I felt terrible as my mind started to clear. A guard set a small stool in the cell for him to sit on.

"Sir," I said, "can you tell me what's going on?"

"Sir? You call me, Sir? I'm really not the best thing to happen to you today."

"I don't know how to act. I've never been in a place like this before."

"I can help you, or I could be your worst enemy. It's up to you. You're being charged with reckless homicide, and that could get you four to fourteen years in a very nasty place. Before I go any further, do you have your own lawyer?"

"Of course not. How do I get one?"

"Just call one you know. He'll direct you to the right kind of lawyer, or have your folks get one for you."

My folks!!! I'd been so wrapped up in my own misery I hadn't even thought of them. "My folks live a hundred miles away. Do they have to know about this?"

"You're old enough to do this on your own, but I'm sure your local newspaper will pick up on this story. Maybe already has."

"You can stop that, can't you?"

He shook his head. "We can assign you a Public Defender if you can't afford a lawyer for your defense. If you want us to."

I slumped back onto the mat, three inches off the floor, and leaned against the block wall. I ran my hands through my matted hair, shook my head, and said in a defeated voice, "I don't know the first thing about this stuff. Do my folks really have to know?"

"How are you going to hide it from 'em, son? You're being charged with reckless homicide. That's the killing of another person while driving drunk. In this case it was a mother of two children, a girl and a boy, aged eight and nine. Do you understand how serious that is? You'll need your family to stand by you."

I killed a person. I killed a mother. Hunter Lowe killed someone. The thought of me killing someone kept clawing at me. "How did that happen so fast? Were others killed or hurt in the accident?"

"Her husband is okay. The two kids were hurt, one seriously, but she'll make it. Her right leg was crushed. She'll keep it, but maybe always walk with a limp."

The nightmare wouldn't stop. In just a few hours my life had turned to ashes. I didn't want Mom and Dad or Gwen to know. But they'd find out somehow.

"Mr. DeSalvo, what's next?"

"It's mostly up to your lawyer and you how you want to plead. Guilty or not guilty."

"I'm guilty, aren't I? I hit that car, I killed that woman ... didn't I?"

He put his hand on my shoulder and gave a light squeeze. Looking at me right in the eyes he said, "I really can't answer those questions, Hunter. Those answers must come from you and your lawyer."

All my life I never drank, mostly thanks to my respect and love for Gwen. Now I'd killed a woman and crippled a little girl. My mind literally hurt and spun in circles. *Guilty or not guilty. That's a dumb thought. I did the crime. Mom and Dad will know. Gwen will know. Friends will know. Have to get a lawyer. My job is over. How will I ever get through all this arrest and jail stuff? Where's my car? Who cares for me around here, anyway? I don't believe all this is going on.*

DeSalvo spoke up and interrupted my thinking. "Tomorrow you'll stand in front of a judge for your first hearing." As he was leaving the cell he asked again, "Hunter, do you want me to arrange for a Public Defender for you?"

"Yeah, yeah, I guess so. He'll just pick up the case and

defend me, huh? Even thou he doesn't know me?"

"That's his job. He does it all the time. He'll get to know you quite well and he'll do his best."

I could see he was trying to leave, probably had lots of other things to do. "Mr. DeSalvo, thanks for your help." Again, he was surprised to see me offer my hand for a handshake.

"I wish I could help you more, Hunter. You seem to be a good kid, but we're on opposite sides from now on."

I felt like he had almost been a friend, but not anymore.

Chapter Five

When my talk with DeSalvo was over, the guards took me to another room and watched me take a shower. What a sickening experience. Even before I was dry they tossed a jail uniform at me, and said, "Here, put this on."

It was like a bad pair of pajamas with the old jailhouse three inch black and white horizontal strips. I thought that outfit went out with the Keystone Cops.

Then they took me to the booking area just like I'd seen in so many movies. One of the first things they told me was that when I was brought in I had a point one two alcohol level, far too high for a first time drunk. How they got the reading, I have no idea. Just like so many other events of that night.

Fingerprinting, mug shots, and questions. Oh the questions. They seemed to go on forever. By this time I felt I had my head on straight and I knew it would be better for me to cooperate with them. It might help me in the future in this place.

They took me to another cell where the rest of the morning dragged on with too much time to think how I messed up so many lives. I don't remember the last time

I cried, but being alone in the cell gave me a chance to bury my face in a pillow so I wouldn't be noticed by the busy people around me. A lot of noisy talking bounced off the echoing concrete walls. Constant opening and echoing slamming cell doors broke up my thoughts. Blaring rock music and some small town trading post program on radio just added to the new and terrible confusion I felt.

At about 11:00 a.m. a drunk was thrown into the cell like another sack of grain. Sort of like how I got here. He only wanted to sleep. The place was peaceful to him.

At noontime, the guard brought us each a bag lunch from Burger Boy down the street. No choice, but after eighteen hours without food it tasted good. The drunk didn't want his, so I devoured his lunch too.

I didn't want to face the world, so I lay there on the bunk with my face to the cold, stone block wall. I looked deeply into the pores of the concrete blocks and slid my finger along the smooth mortar joints.

A guard's loud and commanding voice snapped me back to reality. "Lowe, your dad is here to see you."

The nightmare exploded again. My heart froze instantly like a block of ice. I wanted to throw-up. "Dad?"

I rolled over on the bunk, hoping to drop off the edge of the earth. No such luck. Dad stood at the bars with a face looking like he'd taken a beating. In a way I guess he had. I'd never, *never* seen Dad even sniffle at a disappointment. Now he was reaching through the bars and weeping. I ran to his open arms and didn't stop until my face was wedged between the cold steel bars. We hugged as much as the iron barrier would let us.

"How did you find out?" I asked quickly. "Do the others know? Does Gwen know?"

Tears drenched both of our faces. "Dad, I don't know how all this happened. I'm sorry, so sorry. How are Mom and Sis? Oh, what must Hanna think of her big brother now? Dad, do you know I killed a woman? Dad, I don't want them to see me like this. Is all this real or some stupid nightmare?"

The same questions kept banging away in my skull. "How are Mom and Hannah taking this? Do Gwen and the guys know? Are the neighbors talking?"

"Son, you know our neighbors, they like you. I've called Bruce Cunningham and told him. He's already called Gwen and Aaron. Take this a day at a time. You've got great friends, and they're not going to let you down."

"Don't let them see me like this." My voice began to crack and rise in pitch and I started to break down as shame and guilt took over my speech. "I want you to stay here, and yet I want to be alone. Dad, I don't know what I want. Do you know anything about the other family?"

A guard came up to Dad and said, "Time to go, Mr. Lowe." His voice was as cold as the bars.

"Can he stay a little longer, officer? He just got here. Can we go to a visiting room?" I asked.

"He's been here long enough. No visiting room for you."

They treated my dad with the same criminal attitude they treated me. I felt there was no reason for that.

For the first time in my life I can remember, dad

showed me some physical emotion of love. He kissed my forehead and then stepped back. He said in a choking voice, "I'll get a room for the night and be with you at the hearing tomorrow."

He turned and walked away with shoulders so bent and stooped it looked like there was a knife between them, a knife with my name on it. The bars of the cell door pressed hard against my chest. I wanted to run to him like I did when I was a child, but I was in jail, I was in jail. Little kid stuff was gone.

My very soul exploded in heaves, and I wished with every bone in me that I could hold Mom and Hannah, touch Gwen's silky hair, and feel the trust and support of my two best friends in the world, Aaron Bates and Bruce Cunningham.

"You must be new at this, kid." The other inmate said as he watched me. I just looked at him. I didn't know how to talk to a prisoner.

In all my twenty-three years I had never felt such loneliness, hurt, depression, and guilt all churned up within me. My very soul felt heavy, dry, raw, and hollow. Every breath I took seemed to scorch my lungs. I wondered if my life would be as empty in the future as it had been full in the past. The long nightmare was continuing without a let-up, coming into focus as wicked reality. Would anyone ever speak to me again? Would I ever have a friend? *If my family and friends can't see me, is there anyone who cares for me?"*

No one from the modeling agency had bothered to notify me about my job status. Bart and Jerry hadn't even come to see me. But it was Saturday, so maybe they didn't know about me in this place. Would they ever know?

Monday morning I was handcuffed again and the guards took Dad and me across the street to the courthouse. It was embarrassing to be walking in public in that black-and-white stripped pajama, handcuffed between two guards.

We stood in the street waiting for cars to pass – cars with innocent kids looking at me from the windows. I felt humiliation dripping off me. I'm glad this wasn't happening back home. We went to an empty courtroom with a table in the center where I met Mr. Bronson, the Public Defender. He was a young law school graduate, and told us this was his first job in Sango County. Not very encouraging. Dressed like DeSalvo he reminded me of the suits I modeled in, but his suit didn't come up to the quality I owned or as good as the ones I modeled in.

Entering the courtroom, it looked like a bad TV show with me the prisoner. There were only eight of us in the big room with dark paneled walls, a short wall separating several benches and the two large tables closer to the judge's tall desk. There was a jury box with twelve silent leather chairs. The few windows high on the walls had a lot of Xs as moldings. The whole place smelled like someone had just polished the furniture.

Mr. Bronson explained court procedure to me. "After introductions," he said, "there are several ways this could go. By the way, guard, please remove the cuffs. I don't think we need them."

I was only in the cuffs for just a few minutes, yet when they came off it felt so good. I said, "Thank you," and again I got a look of surprise from the guard.

Mr. Bronson continued. "Mr. Lowe, this could go anywhere from probation to fourteen years in prison. But in all likelihood because of the DUI, running a red light, the death of a woman, the way you treated the officers at the scene — and at the jail the next morning — I'm sure this judge will give you some prison time. He hates drunk drivers, especially young drunk drivers."

Yeah, drunk drivers. Hunter Lowe is one of those now.

Dad and I held each other's hands across the table. Dark clouds of the future rolled in. Mr. DeSalvo came in and took his place at the other table. He looked at me with the sympathetic look that might have said, "I wish I could help you, but my job is to prosecute you."

Chapter Six

When the judge entered, we all stood up and he took his place in a large black leather chair behind the high desk. A uniformed bailiff stood next to him. I found myself standing in front of a judge in an old fashioned jailhouse uniform from the old west. I don't know why, but I thought *the only thing missing in this picture is a rope, a ball and chain, and a shovel.*

"Well, this is a good looking young man. What do we have here, a movie star?" the judge said.

I looked at Mr. Bronson for an answer.

"No, your Honor, this is Hunter Lowe."

"Young man," the judge continued, "I see you are being charged with reckless homicide. What do you have to say for yourself?"

Taking a deep breath and wringing my hands, I said, "Sir, I can't say I'm sorry enough. I'd give up everything I owned if I could have that evening over again to do differently. I've never been drunk in my life. I'm just so sorry, so very, very sorry for the other family. Honestly, sir, if I knew better words to use, I would."

"All the sorries in the world can't give that mother

back to her little kids, can they? Just so you know what's going on, those kids will bury their mother tomorrow, and the little girl will be there in a wheelchair. You know you're in deep weeds, don't you?"

I wanted to hang my head down, but Mr. Bronson told me ahead of time, "Don't take your eyes off the judge when talking to him."

"Yes, sir, I do."

"Drunk driving is the scourge of this city," the judge said in the voice of disgust. "First time or not, I'm not going to let you forget the pain you've caused. I'm setting bail at one hundred thousand dollars, with twenty percent of that up front. As nice of a guy as you seem — now, I want you to stay in jail and start paying your dues."

I heard the gavel slam onto the desk so hard it made me jump. It hurt my ears and I can still hear it. I saw Dad lower and shake his head in disbelief. I'm sure he was wondering where such money would come from. Sure, I had a good job and made a lot of money, but I spent it all at the same time. I lived in a nice condo, and my fancy sports car cost more than I should have spent. And now I can't even drive it. I heard it was totaled. Totaled and "taken care of," I was told. What about all the insurance I paid for? Did the insurance company just write it off and not let me know anything about it? What else is new in this legal septic tank? I never heard from anyone about my job. Just a week ago C.J. told me I was one of his best models, responsible for many accounts. Now no word from him or those two so-called friends from Friday night. Last week we were friends. Now I guess this is what nothing feels like.

"I'm ordering the case to go to the Grand Jury," the judge said. "They can make their decision on a trial."

The lawyers began to pick up their papers.

"Mr. Bronson, could we all get together and talk some things over?" I asked, as we were walking out of the courtroom.

He and Mr. DeSalvo agreed, and within a half hour we were at another table somewhere, and I was ready to speak my mind on what I wanted to do.

Looking at Dad and putting my hand on his arm, I said, "Forget the bail money. I really don't want to go back to Ravenswood at this time anyway. I'm twenty-three, and I've got to be fully responsible for my own poor judgment. I just want to get this mess over so I can get back to work." I turned to the lawyers. "I'd plead no contest, or even guilty, if I could avoid a trial. Just get this over with."

Dad had to leave after the hearing to get back to work. There was nothing for me to do but wait for what the judge, lawyers, grand jury, and whoever else was now in control of my life had their say. I had no idea how long all that would take.

I was returned to the county jail where I started thinking about the coming weeks in a cell, with nothing to do. It just about drove me nuts. The magazines and other reading stuff they let me see only showed the ugly side of life and didn't do anything for me. The worst part was that I had time to think about what the dead woman's family was going through, and what her husband must be thinking. I wondered if there would ever be a way I could face him and tell him how miserable I felt.

I had time, too much time, to think about my childhood, the hopes and dreams of my school days, and about all my friends. What kinds of stories were floating about me back home in Ravenswood? *I hear Hunter Lowe is in jail in Capital City. Never thought I'd hear that.* Was everyone back there talking about me, or did I just disappear out of their minds? Thinking, thinking, thinking, it kept driving me crazy.

To me, sitting on a toilet in a jail cell with no privacy has got to be the lowest and most humiliating experience in life. One perfectly avoidable mistake on my part and here I was — a criminal. I bought into the dumbest and most stupid statement of mankind: "Come on, a couple of beers never hurt anybody."

Later that same day in the county jail, as I was mulling over my dismal future, a strange-but-true moment put a new spin in my life. One of the guards said I had a visitor waiting for me in the courtyard. Courtyard was a nice name for an area of trampled down and worn out grass, a scrawny excuse for a dying tree, all surrounded by walls with barred windows. With an old picnic table painted with bird droppings in the center, it now was a counseling center. Out there, I met a nicely dressed middle-aged man in a turtleneck sweater and a blazer.

"Hi, Hunter, I'm Pastor Ralph Johnson from City Center Church here in Capital City. Your girlfriend's pastor from the Evangelical Church in Ravenswood asked me to visit you."

"News is getting out, isn't it?" I said as I shook his hand.

He nodded. "Gwen's pastor and I went to the same seminary in Chicago several years ago, and we've kept in touch. I read about the accident in the local newspaper, but I should tell you that the other family in the accident is from my congregation — the Marshalls."

That turtleneck sweater and blazer showed a touch of class to me, and at the same time I felt instantly comfortable with this visitor. "Please, please, tell the Marshalls how sorry I am. If I can do anything, anything for them, I'd like to know what it would be."

Pastor Johnson nodded. "Ben Marshall is a strong Christian man. He and the children are trying to deal with this in their own way. If I know anything about Ben, he'll contact you sometime. You see, Ben Marshall and I would like to know you better. Tell me about yourself. What was your life like before all this happened? There's no rush. We've got a lot of time. Ouch, sorry about my choice of words, Hunter."

Chapter Seven

I bit my lip. "It's okay, you're right, we do have lots of time." I spread my hands flat across the table like rolling out a map. Flat on the table that is, around what the birds had left. "Come to think about it, it *is* a good story, full of happy memories — until now. Funny where I'm going to start, but I guess you'll understand.

"Granny always took me to Sunday school. I must have been pretty young to start. I can't remember my first day. Every Sunday, like clockwork, Mom would get my sister Hannah and me ready in good clothes, and Granny would come down the back stairs from her little apartment and walk us to a small Baptist church two blocks away. Mom and dad didn't go unless it was Christmas, or when we were in a program. To them, I guess, they literally took Sunday as a day of rest, or at least a day to sleep in."

Reverend Johnson stopped me. "Why do you remember Sunday school?

"Because Sunday school was neat. Hanna and I would meet a bunch of kids we didn't know from the neighborhood or school, and we got to sing songs, make crafty things and hear some of the most fascinating stories ever. Things were different at Sunday school. The teachers didn't make us do things we didn't like, such as arithmetic and spelling. They were always smiling and talking nice to us. I did get into some trouble once, when the kid behind me had a little wind-up monkey. I turned all the way around with my knees on the chair and laughed too much for my own good. The laughter stopped quickly when I felt the strong but aged arms of Mrs. Gustafson spinning me around and reseating me, with emphasis – and a sliver from the scarred-up wooden chair. She didn't see the monkey and the other kid got away with the trick. I was only seven, and embarrassment ran all over me. But that monkey sure was funny – almost worth the crime.

"One of the things I remember the most about Sunday school was the different little songs we sang. Songs about fishing, building a house, how the sun shines from heaven, and how I'm supposed to be careful about what I see or where I go. I guess *Tommy's Tap* was one of those places, huh? Come to think about it, every one of those little songs has a lot of meaning for growing up. Too bad I didn't catch on at the time."

Pastor Johnson grinned and nodded his head in agreement. "Go on, Hunter."

"Sometimes we'd sing a song like we were talking to Jesus, asking Him to come into our hearts. Almost every Sunday we sang *Jesus Loves Me*. I just clutched the sides of that old wooden chair, slivers and all, swung my feet back and forth not really understanding what some of the songs meant. We sang them just because Mrs. Gustafson said so. Seems like another world away now."

The pastor shook his head up and down. I got the feeling he'd heard this line somewhere before.

"When I was eleven, and Hanna was nine, Granny got sick and died suddenly. Her funeral was at that little Baptist church. I remember a lot of people hugged Hannah and me, but they didn't hug Mom and Dad. The folks seemed uncomfortable around Pastor Lang and the other people, because they were telling them about the church, Sunday school and even things about Hannah and me they didn't know.

"Going to Sunday school ended the same week Granny died. Hannah and I asked Mom several times why, and she said that she and Dad didn't think it was all that important. Soon we got used to sleeping in, and watching Sunday morning cartoons on TV. Mom and Dad were great people though, don't get me wrong. They took us on vacations, and came to all our school events. We had fun doing lots of things as a family. Dad attended as many of my little League games as he could, and his interest in my sports went clear through high school baseball where I did pretty well.

"Junior high school soon became the important thing to me because I always had lots of friends, − boys and girls. I became more interested in the subjects because the teachers paid a lot of attention to me. The lady teachers hugged me a lot, which I thought was kind of funny, but I liked it because it reminded me of how Granny hugged me. They talked to each other about how cute I was. What did I know? I also liked school, because I was always picked early for games and sports, as well as for big parts in the plays and special events. Most of all, I was invited to all the parties."

Suddenly I stopped. "You sure you want to hear all this?"

"Sure, keep going, I'm learning a lot about you. I'm picking something up here," he said.

"Well, okay. When it came to high school, Aaron Bates and Bruce Cunningham and I always hung out together as good buddies. We were known as the Odd Musketeers. Aaron was the funny guy, short and chubby. Okay, truth-be-told, more than just chubby: he was fat. He worked part time at the local Burger Boy but ate there full time. He dressed kind of frumpy and he had a hard time keeping his shirt tucked in. He loved his old greasy baseball cap and wore it somewhere between sideways and backwards. He only removed it when teachers told him he had to take it off. Bruce and I kidded him about getting an oil change on it.

"Bruce was about as different from Aaron as he could be. Tall and even gangly, you could say, he reminded me of the type of people that artist Norman Rockwell painted. His clothes always seemed too short. He was a lot more serious than Aaron, but always had a quick comeback when needed. Bruce and I had birthdays just one day apart, so I guess we were in the hospital nursery together filling diapers. He had long hair and a bad acne problem.

"I fit into this trio somewhere in the middle. They

told me I was the right size and my clothes always were good and fit just right. They also thanked me for keeping girls around us. It was a good picture of how opposites attract. We were just good friends, and happy to have each other. In all the years since high school, I have never known such close friends."

Chapter Eight

At this part of my story, another inmate, my cellmate really, whom I only knew as Nick, joined us at the table. Other than Bruce, Nick was the skinniest guy I ever saw. His arms and neck were loaded with tattoos showing from under the stripes of his jailhouse pajamas.

"Can I get in on this story, reverend?"

"Sure," Pastor Johnson said. "That okay with you, Hunter?"

I nodded. I learned quickly to be frank and honest in this human kennel. "In high school we heard all the lectures and saw the videos against smoking, drinking, careless sex, and drugs. It made common sense to me. Aaron and Bruce started to smoke early in high school, and tried to get me to join 'em. Even though my own folks smoked, every time I tried I could never get beyond one cigarette. After just one week I 'officially' quit. Later, beer became the quest for our bunch. For the same reason that I laid off the cigarettes, I quit with the beer. I couldn't see the point. Neither of them tasted great, and I could never figure out why some people enjoyed them. As for the sexual stories, my friends bragged about their conquests and adventures. Not having those experiences made me the odd ball I guess, but no one really pressed me. Somehow I felt comfortable with not getting into this stuff. I felt better about myself.

"Even though I never got into the smoking, drinking, drug, and the girl chasing crowd, I always seemed to be surrounded by friends. Even the faculty seemed to favor me. Many times I had arguments with friends, and a sort of selfish opinion on a lot of issues. Once in a while someone would call me egotistical, self-centered, and 'pretty boy.' I never knew what that 'pretty boy' remark was all about until one day Mr. Hall, the history teacher, asked me to come to his room after school. 'Nothing serious, you're not in trouble. Just stop by after school before baseball practice, will you?'

"Mr. Hall looked to me how I think John Adams must have looked. You know, our revolutionary hero. He was a short stubby man with a slight New England accent and lots of hair on the sides of his head, with a bald area in the center. He always wore a gray suit and brown shoes. He really knew his history and had a wonderful way with getting that into the thick skulls of high school kids. Also a bit eccentric in his thinking but so very honest and friendly. We all liked him. So after school I walked into his room and he started talking about some strange things. 'Hunter, you've known a lot of attention around here, haven't you?'

"I gave that a little thought, and shrugged. 'Yeah, I guess I have.'

"'Sometimes you have stormy arguments with your

best friends, but they stick with you, don't they?'

"I just sat backwards in one of those classroom desks I'd scooted up to his, wondering what Mr. Hall was getting at. Then he said something that straightened my spine and sort of scared me.

"'Hunter, I'm going to say something intensely delicate and private to you, but I don't want you to think I'm too personal or out of bounds.'

"A bit worried what he was thinking, I slid my desk back a few feet. He snickered and said, 'Relax, Hunter. This is difficult to say, so I'll get right to the point. On a handsome or good-looking scale of one-to-ten, you'd be a twelve. You're handsome to the point of distraction.'

"What do you mean by 'distraction?'

"'Ask some of the girls who lurk in the corners or have your picture up in their lockers.'

"I pulled my head back and lowered my chin. My mind found no connections. I stood up and walked to the window while I tried to figure out where he was coming from or where he was going.

"'Think about it, Hunter. You're always surrounded by people. You've got a good-natured personality. You can be funny or serious depending on any situation. People just want to be around you, even after some sharp disagreements.'

"When I was listening to him I wondered to myself, where's this guy going? What's he up to?"

"'You've never been turned down for a date or dance.' Mr. Hall continued without a pause. 'Your good reputation floats in front of you. Your moist deep blue eyes look like you just stepped out of a shower, and I hear that your dark blond hair with that stubborn wisp of hair lying on your bronzed forehead is the talk of the girls' locker rooms. You're not a short guy like some of us. You're tall enough to stick out in a crowd and carry a muscular body. Not a white tooth out of place, skin as perfect as a Greek god, and you've never had a zit. Your hair is gelled just right, and you wear all the right clothes fitting you like they were tailored to your physique. My gosh, Hunter, look at yourself. Looks like Michelangelo chiseled you out of granite himself. When the good Lord handed out attributes, He threw 'em all at you. You excel in sports, drama, and even get good grades. One more thing, your deep resonating well developed voice is the talk of the faculty lounge. Teachers like to hear you give oral reports. They say you sound like an FM radio announcer. Don't you get that picture of yourself?'"

I was just about to tell Pastor Johnson what happened next, when I remembered where I was in real time. I found myself walking around in circles in the jail courtyard wearing those ugly jailhouse pajamas and he was sitting at the picnic table with the other inmate, hanging on for the next words. "You really want me to go on?"

"Good," Pastor Johnson said. "How did that make you feel?"

"Yeah, go on, how'd you feel?" Nick asked. "I've never heard this kind of stuff before."

I sat back down on the bench, "Well, instantly I felt kind of good, but like a freak at the same time. I walked to the window again and gazed out at the new springtime leaves on the trees. I had a new appreciation for Mr. Hall. No one had ever stepped so far into my comfort zone to speak that privately to me. I didn't think Mr. Hall was making a move on me. Now, of course, I can see he had my interests at heart, but I guess I was right to be a little suspicious when a man says something like that. Anyway, turning around I said, 'I guess I should be lucky, huh? I never thought of all that before. Those things do make some kind of sense.'

"Then he said, 'Hunter, have you ever thought of using your gift as a model or an actor? The folks at Baker's Department Store where you've done some modeling for them in the local paper might have the right idea.'

"'I don't see that as a lifestyle for me,' I said. Then, still looking out the window, giving that idea some space, I heard Mr. Hall say, 'Think about it, Hunter. You really might have a future in it.'

"I turned around with moist eyes and looked straight into Mr. Hall's green irises. 'What do you think I should do?'

"He reached up, put a hand on my shoulder, and simply said, 'Be careful how you treat yourself and others. Continue to be the good kid you are, and hurry off to baseball practice. Coach Harry is waiting for his star pitcher.'"

"Not many people would tell you what Mr. Hall did," the pastor said. "But he was right. Didn't you know that about yourself? That you had exceptionally good looks? Good thing your face was not cut up in the accident. You can get back into the modeling business when all this is over."

"I don't say guys are good looking, but I gotta say you are. You're the lucky one. The rest of us just take the dumb looks we're given," Nick added.

"I guess you guys are right because the modeling was going so well, I have to confess there were times in high school when I did get to thinking I had something others didn't, but then I'd get to feeling conceited and stuck on myself. It made me feel crummy when I thought that way."

"Keep going, what was high school like in your final years?"

"Of all the cellmates I could get," Nick said, "I get Cinderella. Yea, keep going. This I gotta hear. Does it get better? You gotta keep going."

Chapter Nine

"Between my junior and senior year of high school, my friend, Bruce got me a job where he was working on a truck dock, loading and unloading large semi-trucks. The money was better than any of our friends were making, and I called the heavy lifting and sweating my daily workout. I even put on some muscle that summer. It was a no-nonsense type of work attitude, but yet it was a no-brainer as far as the thinking went. I got dirty and sweaty with the best of them, and I learned a lot about life from 'them' truckers and 'da' dockworkers. Some of those lessons I could have lived without. I tried my best to be one of the guys, but they still made snide remarks about my looks and what I could get away with when it came to girls. I saved a lot of money that summer, so I didn't have to work in my senior year of school.

"I was starting to get pretty bummed about this good-looks stuff. One night when Aaron, Bruce, and I were abusing cheeseburgers, fries, and sodas at Jerry's Greasy Spoon. I told them, 'This good-looks stuff is starting to be a curse. Maybe I should find a way to get a cut somewhere, so I'd have some stitches and then a scar on my face or something like that.' Bruce choked on his Coke and Aaron spit out a chunk of cheese, both yelling at me at the same time, 'Gee, that'd be stupid.'

"Aaron went on to say, 'That's a dumb idea, Hunt. If you've got it, flaunt it. I would. It's a great gift. Use it. If I had a face and body like yours, I'd find a way to make money with it. Hey, be one of those, ah, what do you call 'em? Oh yeah, a model.' *I'd heard that somewhere else.*

"At first that idea didn't even sound good to me, but in the weeks to come we talked about it. These two were my two best buddies, and they started to convince me that I should give it a try.

"Senior year in high school brought on all the privileges and fun of being in the top class. Gwen Martin had been my girlfriend for a long time. We finally became an official couple with my ring on her finger, while Aaron and Bruce went out with several different girls that year. All six of us would usually hang out together going to movies, Jerry's Spoon, and school events.

"We began to have the feeling that after so many years of being together in little Ravenswood that the time was coming to a close. Well, it was. Finally Aaron and Bruce got serious about schoolwork. They both hit on the idea that their fair-to-good grades would have to become better if they were going to get into the colleges they wanted. Bruce, in all his blatant honesty, told me that my modeling would lead into acting, TV, and movies, so I'd be financially set into my old age. 'Don't sweat college,' Bruce always said to me. That would be good news to most people I guess, but somehow with all my friends going off to college, and me to a full time job, it just didn't seem right. I was thinking I'd like to go to the college Gwen was going to go to.

"But there was something missing in my life. It was something Gwen would often bring up. She got me to go to church with her once in a while when I was in high school, and it was kind of neat, like grown up Sunday school. Nice friendly people and good music that seemed to say something usually connected with the message. The pastor often referred to the fact that everyone needed Christ in their lives. Personally, I thought with the money, friends, and of course these good looks, what else did I need? What could Christ do beyond that? Did I really miss something there?"

"Hunter, you did. I'm glad you see that now," Pastor Johnson said.

Nick sat up. "I heard that line too, from my priest."

I sighed. "I'm in jail now and who knows what's coming. Maybe I should start looking for what I'm missing."

"Yes, you should. And I could tell you what it is right now," Pastor Johnson said.

For a moment I was unable to speak, but then I said, "I know I should, but I don't think this is the time."

"Don't put it off too long."

"Well, going to church just wasn't as important to me as it was to Gwen. She tried to make me see that I should ask God to have a bigger part of my life, but like I said, I thought that my life was doing just fine with my job and the good money I was making. Sometimes I felt I should

45

have talked to her more about that God thing, but I didn't know where it would go. I could sense disappointment in her attitude, but she seemed to know just when to stop pushing. But the idea of wanting to know more always kept clawing at me like an itch I couldn't scratch.

"I took the guys up on that modeling idea in my senior year. Baker's Department Store continued to ask me to wear some of their jackets, suits, and sportswear in their local ads. I even did a couple of style shows in wedding apparel at the annual Bridal shows around Ravenswood. Style shows were terrible, with all that strutting and funny walking, holding a sad sack face sometimes and a frozen smile other times. It made me feel like a dork if I saw any of my friends in the crowd. They'd make sure I heard them making fun of me. But it was money, and that 'liquid cash' always felt good. I learned later, many of those pictures found their way onto the doors of some of the girls' lockers. Gwen told me some of my underwear ads were on the locker room walls. The ads didn't show my face, but the girls knew it was me. It embarrassed her."

Chapter Ten

From doing all the talking I was thirsty, and when a guard checked on us I asked him if he could get us some water. He grunted and went back inside. It was about ten minutes before he returned with three bottles of water. He almost threw them at us.

Pastor Johnson seemed to be paying attention, but Nick stayed silent. Anyway, once I'd started I found it difficult to stop.

"I was elected president of the senior class, which meant I had all that leadership stuff to do. I hated it. Running meetings, making decisions about little things and speaking to clubs like the local Kiwanis and Lions. I could only do that kind of speaking because of the public exposure I had in modeling, school plays, and of course, the encouragement of Mr. Hall.

"At one particular Kiwanis Club meeting … Hey, you guys don't want me to go on with all this swill."

Reverend Johnson rolled his finger in a circle that said, "Keep going, keep going"

Nick, now slumped over the table, didn't even raise his head as he said, "Yeah, keep going, I'll never hear this stuff again."

"Okay, you asked for it. At that Kiwanis meeting I was introduced as the face of Ravenswood. I was so embarrassed I honestly felt like leaving the room. They all laughed and joked about it. I gave a little speech about our high school and our very successful baseball team that year with my two best buddies as All State Catcher and First Baseman. As a side, I told them that Aaron the catcher was of stocky built, and when he squatted behind home plate I told him he looked like a frog. To get back at me when I was pitching badly, he'd pull down his lower eyelids and rapidly stick his tongue in and out. Bruce, at six foot three and skinny as a Norman Rockwell first baseman, could catch anything we threw at him within nine feet of first base — and still have his big foot on the bag.

"I told the Kiwanis group a few things about the upcoming school play, including the part that I had in it — the village idiot called Squeak. I gave them a sample of the squeaky, high pitched dialogue in the voice of Squeak, and they got quite a kick out of it. While they were all laughing I asked them to buy a bunch of tickets. They thanked me with good applause, and the ticket thing worked. They bought a lot of them.

"After that meeting a sharply dressed visitor from another Kiwanis Club in Capital City came up to me and introduced himself as Dale Anderson, the president of *Future Enterprises.* That was a modeling and entertainment firm that served as an agency for placing young people in such careers.

"He said, 'By watching your mannerisms and listening to you speak in your deep voice and the Squeak voice, I'm sure we could help you in one of our areas, but I'm not going to be the pushy guy that gets you into something you don't want. Please have the courtesy to give us the first opportunity to help you if that's the direction you'd like to go. Here's my card.'

"Mr. Hall, who was now Vice Principal, was standing close. He said, 'Hunter, let's talk some things over before you decide on anything.' Again Mr. Hall impressed me as a person who cared and someone I could trust.

"Back at school in our senior year the usual scene in the guys' locker room was banging lockers, snapping wet towels, and the occasional indecent act. The subject of sexual conquests would often come up, and it wasn't long before I was dragged into the conversations with, 'Hey, Hunt, how 'bout you and Gwen?'

"I would usually say something like, 'I don't creep in your gutters. Or, 'Mind your own business and I'll mind mine.'

"It got so common they'd mock my answers, 'I don't creep in your gutters.' I'd drop or change the subject as soon as I could.

"Gwen was a breath of fresh air wherever she went. I knew her way back in the Happy Hands preschool sandbox. When we were in high school I learned what it was to love someone, and that led us to be a steady couple. She was a part of my heart, and I did everything I could not to hurt her or give her a cause to doubt me. She dressed neat and sharp, but never over the edge. She was

49

always smiling and considerate of others. Because of her Christian witness she played a big part in the reason I didn't drink, smoke, or push her into something she didn't want.

"As far as that sex question between Gwen and me, that was settled as a result of an experience of some friends. Becky Benning was a close friend of Gwen's. Becky and Steve Benson were a couple we often went out with together as a foursome. They were fun to be with and both were high honor students. All of a sudden their relationship seemed to grow cold, and Becky was not her usual bubbly self. It wasn't long before the ugliest of rumors became known. Becky was pregnant. In the locker rooms Steve was the hero, but when Steve and Becky met in the halls she would hang her head, and he'd look like a worm.

"Hey, there I go again, running off at the mouth. What has all this got to do with where I am right now?"

"I should have gone back to the cell a long time ago," Nick said. "But for some reason this is kinda interesting. Hey, I just thought of something. With a story like that and the way you tell it, and with your good looks, ya should have asked for a jury trial. A few winks to the chicks in the jury box and you would have been free in minutes."

"I never thought of that angle."

Chapter Eleven

Pastor Johnson and Nick were clearly interested in my life and told me to keep going. Once in a while a guard would check on us, and because we were not bothering anyone they left us alone. One of them returned to the cell block with his hand opening and closing like a quacking duck, saying, 'Blah, blah, blah.'

"I feel sort of good going over this, I wonder if I'll know good days like that again."

Nick was into the story at this point. "Keep going. Something sounds familiar here. What did that Becky chick do?"

"Gwen would tell me how awful Becky felt, and how she was being pushed aside and left out a lot of things by so-called friends. Steve started to go out with other girls, kind of seedy ones, who thought he was really something. Becky soon became so depressed she had to drop out of school and become a homebound student. I could tell after that if I ever made any moves on Gwen, I'd be a piece of history on the spot.

"Gwen was known as a 'religious' girl because she was always bold and free enough to tell others about her faith, and straighten them out on this 'religious' word. To her, Christianity wasn't a religion, it was a relationship – a personal relationship with Christ.

"Prom time came around, and for the first time in my life I lost a vote. Gwen was voted Prom Queen, and Phil Kish was voted Prom King. As they danced the 'King and Queen Dance,' I watched from a distance as the one I loved was in the arms of another. I knew it was only for a few minutes, but my loss must have shown because Bruce, in all his candor, was quickly at my side. 'Well, friend, how does it feel to lose one, huh? Just like the rest of us.' I looked at him in a startled way. Then seeing that grin on his face, I smiled and poked him in the cummerbund. 'What would I do without a friend like you?'

"As president of the senior class I had the honor of reading the name of the students as they came up for their diplomas at graduation. As I read each name – most of them I knew since kindergarten – I couldn't help but feel that this was truly the last time we'd all be together. The breakup had already begun. Becky was 'showing,' and the stuffy superintendent didn't think it would be proper to have her there for the graduation ceremony. I had to skip her name. Reading the name Steve Benson, the next one on the list, sounded like a hollow thud. There was no cheering as he walked to get his diploma. Just silence that told us all what the class thought of him.

"If you guys are still here, I'll finish this trip down memory lane."

With his head resting in his hands, Nick just nodded.

"Shortly before graduation, Mr. Hall and I talked about what Mr. Anderson offered at the Kiwanis meeting. He said, 'I've known Dale Anderson for a long time, and I know him as an honest and upright man. He can introduce you to a lot of opportunities that I think could be exciting.'

"'But college, Mr. Hall,' I said. 'Don't you think I should go to college like the rest of the guys?'

"He shrugged his shoulders. 'I know it would mean moving a hundred miles away from here, and about 325 miles from where Gwen is going to school, but it isn't the end of the world. If you don't take advantage of the invitation now, you could regret it later. It would pay well, and if you wanted to go to college after a few years you could easily do that. Better yet, you could model part time and keep paying for school. My gosh, Hunter, you stand where thousands of young people would like to be standing – including me. You have a great gift. Use it while you can. You never know what the future holds.'

"With that advice, and encouragement from Mom, Dad, Hanna, Gwen, Aaron, and Bruce, I called Mr. Anderson a week later. Within two weeks I was starting a modeling career. Classes on dressing, walking, smiling, motivation, and speaking filled my days and most evenings. I had a hard time learning to strut myself, and pose so everyone would look at me. Learning how to force a smile and still make it look natural was harder than I thought. I also learned to keep a serious face even though funny things were going on in the audience. I found out all too quickly that the modeling business is more than just clicking cameras and flashing lights. The hours were long, and so much posing over and over and over got boring. Genuine smiles got harder.

"The demands of the schedules and fast changing of clothes really got tiring. The directors thought nothing of just continuing shooting as long as they wanted to. We were always thinking about the end of the day and quitting to getting something to eat. Mr. Anderson's agency was more concerned about pleasing the client than making us into for celebrities, so none of us were very well known, although some of us did make it to magazine covers.

"The agency also had a continual schedule of shooting for their Internet service: faces, poses, and subjects for thousands of situations. All a customer had to do was dial up our website for a certain picture and situation. Many times we traveled around the world for pictures on location. Never first class though, and the hotels were in the one broken star category. As time went on, the backgrounds were often put in with the aid of computers using a green background for us, so the traveling got less and less.

"I modeled everything from underwear to overcoats, sandals to baseball caps, toothpaste to men's jewelry. I had my picture taken in some of the finest clothes, sports equipment, cars, motorcycles, and boats you could think of. I spent two years almost constantly on the go. For a while I modeled exclusively for a nationally known catalog and certain clothing labels. We even had a workout room where we had to spend up to two hours a day running and lifting weights. The best part was that we got paid for working out. The money was getting better all the time, and I was often called on for more jobs than some of the other guys.

"This must sound self-serving for me to be talking like this, but you keep telling me to go on."

"Yeah, don't stop now. You gotta be coming to an end soon," Nick said.

"There was little time for Gwen and me to be together. She was in college, also working hard, so we decided to invest these few years into making some money to set aside for our future. Just about two months ago the agency got me into a series of TV commercials. I did some work for large industrial manufacturers in their advertising brochures and training DVDs. As fun as the job might seem to others, I got to thinking again that there was a hole in my life. I sure wanted to know how Gwen found so much peace in her faith. I wasn't always as happy as my pictures showed.

"After one especially rough day and evening of shooting, a group of us went to *Tommy's Tap,* like we often did, where I always had a Coke or some other soft drink. My friends constantly made fun of me, but I was sure of myself and didn't mind. On that night, for some unknown perfectly dumb and brainless reason, I fell for that ignorant line, 'A couple beers never hurt anybody.' Well, a few beers in me and that's where that lady's life ended. And so did my story and life. Now I'm in this kennel. Reliving my high school years showed me just how much I lost at that bar.

"Reverend Johnson," I said, while reaching for his hand. But I choked up and had to wait.

The pastor nodded in understanding.

I regained my composure. "Do you think there's any hope for me in the future?"

"I'm in the business of seeing great things done in broken lives, Hunter. You're no exception. After all you've told me, I'm sure the Jesus you learned about in Sunday school, and who Gwen tried to introduce you to, has big plans for you. I don't know what they are now, but the Jesus I know does things in a big way."

"That go for me too, Preacher?" Nick said quietly.

"Yes, Nick, God cares for you too."

Chapter Twelve

During those two weeks in the county jail, I had time to collect my thoughts and attitude. I almost begged the guards to let me do something, anything to step out of the cell for some time. When they discovered I was serious about doing anything, they put me to work doing some of their routine and detested jobs.

Other inmates got on my case and spent most of their time laughing at me and calling me the maid, or worse things. I really didn't care. I found some purpose in doing something worthwhile as I waited for the result of the hearing. I thought any of this nice guy stuff would help me with the judge's decision.

Within those two weeks, I guess the guards even felt a little friendship with me. They let me wear one of the new orange jumpsuit uniforms they were trying out. I was glad to be out of the baggy zebra pajamas. I also felt they could trust me with things they would not usually trust other inmates to do. When they told me I could clean and wash the cars out in the sally port, my first question was, "Who's Sally Port?"

A guard said, laughing, "It's not *who* is Sally Port, it's

where is the sally port. That's the place where the cars are parked when we bring you guys in. You'd probably call it a garage, but we call it the sally port."

"Why that name?"

"A sally port is a secure entrance to someplace. Old forts and castles had these at the entrance. I've heard it's an early nautical term. It has always been called the sally port ever since I've been here."

After I got to working in the sally port I always saw that I was locked securely within the compound. I never thought police cars could be so cruddy inside. There were so many things to clean in them: the separation cage, computers, leg shackle hooks, junk behind the cushions, donut crumbs, and about five radios. To add to that, there was the vomit some "clients" would leave behind. I sure didn't notice all that on the night I had a ride in one of the cars. I felt sorry for the guys who had cleaned up after me.

One day, when I was feeling a little liberated, I thought I'd have some fun with the sergeant on duty. For some reason of neglect, an officer left the keys in the ignition when he parked the car in the sally port. When I finished washing it, I took the keys to the sergeant, tossed them on his desk and said, "Here are the keys. I've parked the car in the lot."

He choked on his donut and almost fell off his spinning swivel chair. "That's not funny, Lowe. You didn't really drive that car out, did you?"

"No, sergeant. Sorry."

They even let me clean the offices. At first they

enjoyed having someone doing the "maid's job," but they soon became almost friends. Using the words, *let me wash, let me clean*, sure were not the terms I thought I'd ever be saying. But I felt like a free canary getting out of that cage for a few hours a day, although I sure wouldn't get far around town in that bright orange jumpsuit. Just to be able to pick a bucket or broom out of a closet on my own was a privilege. A month earlier I couldn't have imagined finding any pleasure in such a little task.

Never having been in a place like this before, I quickly discovered a lot about life in a jailhouse. When a new inmate was brought in I never knew what to expect. They didn't care how they looked, what they said, what they wore, or how they smelled. I saw what I must have looked like when I arrived. They didn't care how they acted or what clothes they took off. If they had anything small and metallic, like a button on a pair of jeans, they would use it to scratch graffiti on the painted walls or door. Some clawed at the walls like an animal. The worst part was that some would not even use the toilet, just for spite. That's where the guards were glad I was there with their mops.

Two days before the Grand Jury met, Dad, Mom, Hannah, and Gwen came to visit. I never knew what mixed emotions meant until that day. I was tremendously glad to see them, but so ashamed and embarrassed to have them see me in jail. My relationship with the officers had improved by now so they let me wear a new jumpsuit. They also let us have a "picnic" in the center courtyard. They called it a plaza, but it was just the same outside area where Pastor Johnson, Nick and I had that long story about my high school days. It was still surrounded by gray walls and barred windows, with just a few patches of grass struggling to survive and stay green. Nothing worth mowing. Lunch from Burger Boy of course – courtesy of the state – and the afternoon went quite well.

Near the end of the visit, my folks let Gwen and me have a moment to ourselves. Holding her hands and looking into her beautiful eyes, even for a short time, was my most thrilling event of the past month. Alone, I was able to tell her, "Gwen, Gwen, I'm so sorry for embarrassing you and your family. I hope your mom and dad don't hate me."

Her voice was encouraging. "They love you, Hunter. They still pray for you, and so do I. I'm going to stand by you, and in a few years we can pick up our lives again."

Not wanting to let go of Gwen's hands in the cool and breezy shade of the courtyard, I said with soggy eyes, "That could be up to seven years."

"Hunter, I don't care if it takes that long or even more."

With fluttering high pitched words I managed to say, "That's a world away, Gwen." I looked into her innocent face, with blinking eyes, and then forced the most bitter tasting words I've ever said through my lips. "I don't know how or why you should do that. You should find another guy."

"No, never!" she said quickly. "I've known you far too long to let you just fade away. I care about you. I *really do* love you."

I didn't think they would let me hug her, so I squeezed her hands. In the confusion her smile was distant, her eyes welling with tears. But how could it be otherwise? I don't think she knew which way to turn or what was coming next.

Dad returned to Capital City to sit in the courtroom the day my decision was carried out. I told Mr. Bronson I'd rather take a bench trial and not a jury trial. In the negotiations, Mr. DeSalvo and Mr. Bronson agreed to five to seven years, so there was no pre-sentence investigation and no trial. Dad and I were alone with them and I sat with my arms crossed on the table when they broke the news of their decision to me. I sat stunned and screamed within myself, *Five to seven years? Five to seven? O dear God, I didn't think it would be that much. Three or four maybe, but not five to seven.* My head dropped into my arms with a bounce, and I felt the whole disgusting nightmare start all over again. Dad and I were never hugging buddies, but I sure wish he was that day. I needed the strength I'd come to see in him.

To my horror the judge agreed, and transportation was arranged for me to be sent to an intake facility. Life in the county jail was raw, but I was about to learn what prison was really like and which one I'd be sent to. So much for trying to play nice. So much life and air was sucked out of me I couldn't even talk. Even the jail vocabulary I had learned in the past two weeks failed me.

Chapter Thirteen

Regardless of who I was, or whatever possessions I had, I discovered it could all be taken away in an instant. I still had my famous face as some called it. No one could take that away. At least I might be able to go back to my career after this is all over. People care little about the former life of a model or actor. I even thought how interesting it would be to read about my past in one of those tabloids at the checkout lane.

The difference between my first day in the county jail and my last were like night and day. The first day I was treated like a dirty rag, and I now know why. Alcohol in any form is not a friend to man. But on the last day I had friends, from Nick to all the guards.

Four days after the judge agreed to the settlement, the time for me to go was at shift change, and most of the guards from the county jail were on hand to wish me well as I left to go to that intake facility. Their handshakes were tight and sincere. I got the feeling they were concerned for my future and wanted me to know they cared. I was handcuffed, as was usual for transferring an inmate. A large beige charter bus was waiting with

Department of Corrections brazenly printed on the side in black lettering. A van was parked right behind it.

Reverend Johnson stepped up to me and squeezed my shoulder. "Hunter, I promise to keep in touch, and I'm putting you on my daily prayer list."

He gave me a discrete hug and patted me on the back as he whispered in my ear, "Jesus does care for you, and one day you'll find out just how much – big time."

As I stepped up to get into the bus, I could see that I was taking more steps down in my life. The driver and his "shotguns" were anxious to go. Without any more farewells, the hissing of the closing door and releasing of the brake sent me to a new life I knew nothing about.

Inside the bus, I could see a heavy wire mesh separating the guards and the prisoners. A guard guided then pushed me into a front seat of the rear section where ten other prisoners from other jails were already waiting. Two of them looked at me and burst out laughing. I was told, in hard words, to sit down in the front part of the section where someone shackled my legs to brackets in the floor. Another level of self-respect lost.

As the guard was clasping the chains to the floor, he whispered, "Kid, don't listen to them. They'll try and get to you." For some reason I accepted that as almost a kind word of warning.

Just as the bus began to move, the older prisoners started in on me just like the guard said they would. "Hey, Scars, check out the new kid up there. Looks like somebody downstate will have fresh meat soon."

"I don't know what you done to get on this trip, kid,

but you're in for the ride of your life."

I didn't move and kept looking ahead. *If I ignore them they might shut up.*

"Hey, scum, look at us when we talk to you!" one of them yelled.

Because of my good bringing up, I guess, I naturally turned around. As I did, all of them laughed and shook their heads. One said, "You're young and beautiful, but you don't have a clue what's coming, do you?"

The recent good wishes of the guards from Capital City and Reverend Johnson were quickly replaced again by the feeling of sinking into a bottomless pit.

The trip to the intake facility was short, but the way the career jailbirds were talking it was a long ride. *Am I really heading for the abuse I hear about that happens to young guys in prison?*

The Department of Corrections intake facility was where they separated new "clients" from the experienced one. Uniforms of different colors were issued to inmates of various crimes. Some even got the old fashioned white and black stripped ones. They also tried, sometimes unsuccessfully, to separate the gang members, serious racially vocal people, gays, and first offenders. Those who were committed of crimes on children were really treated badly.

From one ordeal to another, we were handcuffed and chained to each other in a long line waiting and waiting for a decision to be made. We looked like a long line of cattle being led into boxcars. I learned later, the guards called it the cattle call. That made sense. After two weeks of feeling like a side of beef I was prodded into another bus for the excursion to Putnam Prison, my new home.

I had often seen these buses on the highways, and wondered what kinds of losers were inside. I found out that day — guys like me. Out the dark windows I could see people gawking at the bus like we were in a parade. The other prisoners in the bus had been through this several times before. On the bus this time these were new guys to me, but they still sang the same song and had choice words for me. I fell lower with each mile.

To occupy my time, I mostly just looked out the window and watched my freedom go by. Left to my own thoughts, I wondered if any drivers and passengers in the cars realized the freedom they had when they traveled along these highways. I also did a lot of wishing of how things would have been different, but I had to discover the hard way that the real world doesn't run on wishes.

I learned the simple fact that I'm totally responsible for what I do, and there's no turning back the clock just because I blew my chances. Looking in the rear view mirror, life may look twenty-twenty, but I didn't have that luxury any longer. I didn't have *any* luxury any longer. I should have learned the bad lessons of life from the mistakes of others. A strange thought hit me: *Are you really with me in this, Jesus?*

I thought of Aaron and Bruce, and in a heartbreaking way I wished they knew what was going on. I sure could use their support in this dead-end bus trip. They were the only two guys in my life I could have hugged right then and shared my deepest thoughts. I'd have settled for the sight of their funny faces or their hands on my shoulders. Maybe they didn't know. Maybe that was for the best. They were busy at two different colleges, but I couldn't help thinking that if they knew what was going on they'd want to do something for me.

We passed a sign that read *Ragged Cliffs State Park*. Was this trip planned to torment me all the way? Just two months ago one of my final photo shoots was in this park. Eight of us were doing a shoot for winter sports gear, snowmobiles and winter hiking equipment. It was in the summer, and sweating was a big problem in heavy clothing. Makeup people had to wipe our faces just seconds before the cameras started to click. There were only a few minutes of shooting at a time before we had to take off a layer of clothing and cool down. Even the changing of all the clothing was done right there in the park, out of camera range. Both the guys and girls, such was the non-privacy of models.

Posing for winter shots in the summer time was fun for us because the support staff always had to work harder and faster than we did. People doing makeup, costumes and lighting, and the producers, were always in each other's way trying to make us look good. It never ceased to amaze me how the computer people could manipulate the pictures of us in front of a green screen and blend in snow all around us to make a hot day in July look so cold in the catalogs.

As the bus drove on past the park I wondered if I would be part of that life again. It had been hard work being a model, but there had been a freedom with it that

I'd not known in the past two months. A freedom where, in my own time, I could come and go as I wished, I could choose my clothes, food, CDs, DVDs, and TV shows. I had lost that freedom, and now I was watching whatever there was left of my life slither past darkened windows. I wished I could press my face to the glass like a little kid, but the little kid in me was gone.

Chapter Fourteen

We stopped at another town on the way to pick up two more prisoners. As they climbed into the bus they took one look at me and both burst out laughing. *What's with all this laughing,* I thought.

The trip continued. All I could do was turn my face back to the window and ignore them. I felt my heart drop another few notches.

As we passed through small town after small town, I'd look out at stores of all kinds that I couldn't walk into anymore. We passed a grocery store where I imagined rows and shelves full of good things to eat – now everything out of reach. Clothing stores, shoe stores, bakeries, and coffee shops faded out of my hopes. I never thought a guy could miss those things. Kids on tricycles, bikes, rollerblades, and skateboards would be off my radar screen, and the beauty of red, orange, yellow, and brown trees of fall would be a thing of the past. Even squirrels chasing each other around would soon be nothing but a memory.

I felt so much of the good and simple things in life sinking out of my sight, not to be enjoyed in the future.

Five to seven years was like a dark and stormy cloud rising over me. Fresh air, breezes, and space would soon turn into ventilated air, concrete walls, cold metal bars, and slamming doors. The county jail in Capital City was bad, but from what the other prisoners and the guards said, Putnam Prison was going to be a lot worse — yet it was just rated as medium.

Near the edge of a town we passed a high school at noontime. Now that really hurt. School buses were parked at the side of the building, with lots of kids milling around. Some couples were sitting on stone walls, others walking, talking to each other and holding hands. That sight alone stabbed my heart. Many times Gwen and I looked forward to our lunchtime together to do just that, hold each other's hand. Oh God, how I missed her touch. How I wished I could hear her voice and even listen to her witness for Christ. I turned a deaf ear to her so often.

The thought of losing Gwen to another guy at college made my lungs feel raw, and breathing was difficult. Maybe Gwen should find another guy. In my tormented mind I could already see some guy making a move on her. I remembered how back at the county jail in Capital City, I had even brought up the subject. I could only blame myself if she did find another guy.

The trip was supposed to take only two hours, but it felt like a slow motion nightmare with too much time to think and watch the wonderful world outside fade away through the darkened windows.

Panic squeezed my chest and I felt I was tumbling

head first through a narrowing, spiral tunnel not knowing what was at the bottom. The thoughts crawling through my mind were like pythons dragging me down into an ever-darkening abyss. I couldn't believe the falling sensation that started the morning I woke up after the accident. It was always with me. I was always falling.

With nothing else to do but think, I got to imagining I was in this bus because the beer manufacturers and advertisers showed a fun and appealing life style for young people using their products. I realized it was all a hideous lie. I had blacked out, totaled my car, killed a woman, destroyed *her* family, devastated *my* family, would probably lose Gwen, and let down the two best buddies I had in the world. Would any salesman, advertiser, or liquor executive offer to help pay any of the expenses for the Marshalls or myself? Would they admit any compliance in the misery their products caused to thousands? Would any of them stand on a porch and tell someone that their sons or daughters were killed because they drank their beer? Would any beer manufacturer dare to defend me or anyone in a courtroom in the trial I went through? I don't think so.

Like a five gallon bucket of cold water being thrown in my face, one of the guards said, "Take a few deep breaths, guys. Here's your new home."

Instinctively I did just that. I took some deep breaths. The other prisoners laughed at me again. I looked to my right and saw a wall, a high ugly old dark brick wall that seemed to say, "Dead end!" all over it.

The two-hour trip from the intake facility to the

prison was over as the bus drove through two sets of gates into a large garage, but I knew it was just a bigger sally port this time. A guard opened the door and we faced other guards holding rifles on us. To think the guns were loaded and pointing at me, took my spirit down even some more notches. The guards shackled all our ankles and wrists together in one long chain. I experienced the depressing, lost, frightened and hopeless feeling a slave must have felt over three hundred years ago when leaving the slave ship. Sunshine and fresh air were slammed shut out of my life.

The greeters were not trained by any of those superstores. Other than, *"Shut up, and follow that guard!"* No one said a word. We just clanked and shuffled our way down a noisy hall. The thought of any of us trying to make a run for it was a big joke. We were prodded and poked with their sticks, and I heard one say, "Here's that cute one we heard was coming. He tried to fight it out with the cops at the accident scene." News travels fast, I guess. "Got to hand it to you, kid, that took some guts. Try it here, and we've got just the guy who'll teach you a few things. In fact he'll teach you a lot of things you never knew. Starting tonight"

I could imagine Gwen back at N.I.C.C. sitting in the library trying to study, her mind working overtime and wandering to thoughts of me. She'd not seen me for three months – except that quick trip to Capital City to the county jail with my folks.

At the time, Gwen wrote to say it had been nice to see me, but she felt the short visit was strained, although a sort of a necessary appointment. I knew she'd made herself keep up a good front, but in the next letter I detected the feeling she was having second thoughts about me. Here I was, a boyfriend in prison, something that never was in the wildest plans for our lives.

In the following letter, Gwen admitted that her visit to me at the county jail rekindled many high school hopes and dreams we'd had for our future, and the touch of my hands had brought back those memories. But she reminded me how I'd said, "You'd better find another guy — you don't deserve me." That was one of those statements I wished I'd never said. The memory of it really hurt. "I'm praying every day about us," she wrote. "I'm praying, 'Jesus, Savior, Friend, what can I do for the one I love?'"

As I read that letter, the name of Erik Hansen kept coming to the front of my mind. She told me he was a tall, blond, sun reddened soccer player at N.I.C.C. All I could think of was that this twenty-three-year-old was just the sort of guy who would take an interest in Gwen now that she was vulnerable. It wasn't long before I convinced myself that Erik's outgoing personality and attention were already starting to chip away at Gwen's defenses.

When he was four years old, Erik had moved to the United States from Denmark with his parents. He still retained a slight Scandinavian accent, which he desperately tried to shake, but the girls at N.I.C.C. thought it was cute — even Gwen. Maybe especially Gwen.

Before the accident, Gwen had turned down many invitations from guys for a date. But just being in college she was associated with many students, half of them guys. She would tell me about this attention when I used to see her before the accident. We even laughed about it, but in a way she seemed to convey the impression she was feeling left out of the college social life by being committed to me. This is the reason I felt I should have gone to college instead of modeling. In classes, walking around the campus and at *Snoopy's* without me — *Snoopy's* was hole-in-the-wall bagel and coffee shop just off campus — these were the things I knew would put a strain on our relationship. At college she was surrounded with activity. But now, with me locked away, surely Gwen was feeling even more left out.

Sure, she'd have friends. Friends were good for her. As long as that's all they were.

Chapter Fifteen

Wednesday of that week was the day I arrived at Putnam Prison to the sound of slamming and banging doors that was to become a part of my life again. I think the guards enjoyed making the steel doors do the intimidating for them.

The warden's name was Mr. Pitts. I thought that was fitting. If his little welcome speech was meant to be motivational, it missed — by a long shot, (pun intended). "If you play by the rules and behave yourself," he said, in a cold and couldn't-care-less monotone voice, "you'll make it out of here and get back to your life."

I thought, *behave yourself?* What does a guy in prison know about behaving?

The other experienced new clients just rolled their eyes, looked at the ceiling, and shifted their weight from one leg to another. The speech was obviously a re-run of many before. He reminded me of the mealy warden in the movie, *Cool Hand Luke.* In fact he even looked like the little chubby guy. There was no real comfort or hope built into the speech. In fact, I thought it was a warning of some sort that sounded more like, "Look out, you ain't seen nothing yet."

We were finally unshackled from each other, strip-searched and handcuffed again, a real picture for the Internet crowd. We were led like cattle to a supply room and given uniforms, shoes, bedding, and a pillow. Trying to hold all that stuff in my arms while in handcuffs was just another example of organized futility. One of the other newcomers dropped a shoe and when he tried to pick it up a guard kicked him in the legs, another clue of the friendly caring sensitivity to come. Next we were finally given the dignity of putting on the uniforms that fit like pajamas and made us look like clowns. Size and fit was not a concern to the supplying inmates.

Nothing fancy from the linen closet either. Just old worn out thin but clean gray sheets. *Washed without detergent I guessed. Don't go there.* Government surplus blankets and a faded blue and white striped pillow without a pillowcase. Just like in the movies. For some unknown reason – who needs a reason for anything here – we were all taken to different cellblocks.

The first thing that hit me when I entered the cellblock was the smell. The odor of weak bleach trying to cover up a mixture of man smells, sweat, urine, and cigarettes almost gagged me. Some inmates were in the hall, others in the commons talking and smoking, while still others were reading paperback books, magazines, or watching TV. It was a scene of idle men roaming in a collection of nothing. I was led down a long row of cells with some doors open and others closed. In the cells that were closed, a few prisoners were trying to sleep. Maybe they were so used to the noise and smell that they really were sleeping. From other cells an ugly assortment of rock, rap, country music, and mid-day talk shows fought to be heard above each other. If I wasn't at the bottom of my life now, I was getting close.

During that walk down the row of cells, I felt absolutely everyone stop what they were doing and stare at me. From inside their cells or from the commons they started to yell at John, the lead guard.

"Going to put him in with *Dog,* John?"

"Don't do it."

"Not that kid, John."

"No, no, no."

"John, have a heart, think about it."

"Put him in here."

"John, think what you're doing."

"We'll get you for this, John."

"Put him in with Tyrone."

"Hey, John, put him in my crib."

Hearing those voices was making me freak out — being the new young guy in prison.

"Look at him, John. For the last time, don't do it, not with Dog!"

We finally arrived at a cell where a burly, tattoo-laden, pony tailed, fat looking gorilla type of a guy stood with hairy knuckles hanging out between the bars. A threatening grin crept out from behind a repulsive beard and broken teeth. *How low can my heart sink?*

"Move away from the door, Charlie," John demanded.

As the other guard took the handcuffs off me, he said, "What I heard about you, from the cops in Capital City, you deserve to meet our Dog. He does the real orientation for us — free of charge for the state."

I never imagined I could have felt worse than I had a few minutes earlier, but now whatever spirit I had left in me was shattered like a broken window. I quickly thought, *the cell is the size of the walk-in closet I had in my condo. Now I have to live in it with this depraved monster.* I continued to feel the falling sensation. John took my chin in his hand, took a close look at my face, and said something I totally didn't understand, yet it riveted my spine straight.

"I'll never see you like this again." With those words he slammed the door shut so loud I can still hear it. Just like the judge's gavel back in Capital City.

I turned around and looked at the grin of an angry and hungry pit bull. He took a long time just looking me up and down. Then he mumbled, "Bottom bunk. Yours. Enjoy. I know I will."

I extended my hand for a handshake, and said, "Hi, my name is Hunter Lowe."

He just looked at my hand and turned around. He grabbed the chain to the upper bunk with one arm and swung his legs up to it. Just like a gorilla. I couldn't believe my eyes.

I tried to talk to him in a general way, but his answers were just a word or a grunt — now I knew something about his level of education. He didn't seem at all interested in my questions. As I put the sheets on my bunk and tried to be civil to him, he kept looking at me and grinning. "Ha, making your bed? Dat don't last."

The only thing in the cramped cell besides a toilet and sink were the bunk beds chained to the wall, some pornographic magazines on the floor, and pictures of naked girls on the walls. This stuff was far from the *Home Sweet Home* collection.

It wasn't long before I heard other cell doors open and inmates step out to get in line for the chow hall.

The inmate in the cell next to me said, "Hey, kid, step out. They throw a bone to Dog in his cage. Guards don't want him in the chow hall with the rest of us."

I followed the line in silence as we went down an iron circular set of stairs to the large, stark, empty and echoing chow hall full of men slouched over their trays. After going through the serving line, I ended up at a table where the guys just looked at me again. Some were talking among themselves, so I said, "Can I speak?"

"Yeah, yeah, kid, what's on your mind?"

"I thought cells had doors on them with small windows. There are just bars around here."

One said, "This is the old way prisons was made, we in one of the oldest joints in the state."

"You'll get used to it. It really ain't all bad. With those solid doors the guards don't know what's going on in them cells. Sometimes stuff ain't all too nice, At least this way everything going on can be seen through the bars."

"One good thing about these open bars is that you seem to have more space around ya than with them doors," another one said.

I bravely asked, "What can I expect around here?"

They all spoke at once.

"I'll tell you one thing. The pit bull where you live now ain't no friend of yours."

"Sleep with one eye open at all times."

"I don't know what you did to get here, but you ain't leaving looking like you do now. I don't say this to no guy, but you look good to all of us."

"So why do they call him the pit bull, or Dog?" I had to ask, as if I couldn't guess what they meant by the term "pit bull." A couple of guys laughed and the others quietly looked down at their food. I heard one mutter under his breath as if he didn't want me to hear it, but at the same time did want me to hear it. "O, my fine looking brother, you'll find out tonight."

With that weak show of encouragement I just picked at my food until I heard a voice say, "Better eat that stuff fast, or the cooks will throw it at you and you'll finish eating it off the floor. Them guys will take it like an insult."

Another voice said, "Can you imagine them being insulted?"

"Nice place you got here." I squeezed out quietly under my breath, wondering, *how much farther do I keep falling?*

When I got back to the cell, Dog was just finishing his turkey cold cuts, and the tray was lying near the door.

"Step on that tray and I'll break your foot." There was no doubt he could, so I walked around it carefully, letting him know I could play nice. I spent the rest of the evening trying to figure out how a person can do so much of nothing in so much empty time without anyone to talk to, even though he was never more than five feet from me.

The whole place suddenly went black as the lights were shut off without any warning. I took that as a hint to go to sleep. I must have lain there for hours wondering what the guys at the table were talking about. After that long and terrible day I was really tired, but I hoped I would never fall asleep. In that twilight time I realized my life had come to nothing but being in this cage with a gorilla I couldn't talk to. It just couldn't get any worse. I didn't know the moment I fell asleep. The next thing I was aware of was a smelly, heavy body laying down on me.

Chapter Sixteen

Instantly I realized what was going on, and felt so repulsed I pushed him off of me as hard as I could, His head hit the wall first, then hit the floor with a *crack* that energized every nerve in his body. Rising up with bugged-out eyes he spit on me. If he'd stopped there I would have been thankful, but he grabbed me by the shirt and had me off the bed in a flash, banging my head on the top bunk on the way up. If this was to be a fight it was over right then and there, it was now a mauling with me, the maulee.

Dog held me with his left hand, and started slapping and punching me in the face like a boxer working out rapidly on his punching bag with his right. My feet were off the floor. I couldn't get any traction to move away. Although I thought I was well built and strong as a result of my high school job at the truck dock, and the weight lifting I did at the modeling agency, his strength was more than twice my efforts. That weight lifting was just for looks. He threw me at the toilet and I remember hitting the edge of it with my right eyebrow. I felt a sharp pain as the skin was ripped open. I could feel blood coming out of the wound. Before I could get up, he grabbed an ankle and spun me around on the floor until I slid spinning in circles across the cell, banging my head into the bars at the front.

I called for help whenever I caught my breath, weak as it was, and I heard other inmates yelling for help at the same time. But, but no guards showed up. With his legs straddling my chest there was another session of punching and slapping. Dog stood me up, and wrapped his big smelly arms around me. I don't think I'll ever forget the bodily stench of that man who had not been close to a shower for a week or more. He bit my left ear and the side of my neck. Dropping me to the floor like a rag doll, he kicked me until I was out of breath again. *Thank goodness it's over,* I thought — wrong again. He kept coming at me.

I was in the presence of raw hate and anger, a demonic force with eyes to match, full of fire and a face of rage. This time when he picked me up, he hung me upside down with my feet wedged between the bars at the top of the door. He tore off my clothes, and then growled, "I hate your face. I hate your face. Here's a new one."

The punching started all over again. I was so weak and helpless my only thought was, *is anyone* ever *going to stop this or will this go on for five years?* While I was hanging there, my ankles searing in pain, he broke some of my teeth with his knee. His strength didn't let up. It knew no limit. With his strong arms grasping the bars, he pressed his whole grimy body against me while he cursed and cursed, and bit me more on the legs. Then he continued to abuse me in ways I never thought were possible. I don't know how Dog could have done so much damage to me in that small space, and in just a short time. Experience, I guess.

Finally, I heard voices and felt the cold water the guards threw at him. When I fell into a heap on the concrete floor, I thought I was in a zoo and the water was the only way to break up a fight between animals. Hence the name Dog, I guess.

With his hands grabbing the chains on the wall, he swung himself back to his top bunk like a wild animal after its kill. I saw him lick my blood from his lips. Lying on the cold floor in all that blood and water, with no clothes on, I knew right away there was no more modeling for me. I would never make a living looking into the front side of a camera lens again. My functioning eye focused on the drain cover and I saw any future hope of an acting career swirling through the grate. I saw blood, hair, skin, broken teeth, tears, and water being sucked out of my life. Even though every blood vessel in my body was throbbing, I was glad this mauling was over. *If this was the first night, what was coming in the next years?*

Like that night in Capital City after the accident, voices began to come clear to me out of the groggy darkness of my mind.

I heard the door slide open and one guard say to the others, "I wish John wouldn't put young kids like this in with Dog, just to have him do this to them. Did you see this kid today?"

"Well they do learn fast, thanks to Dog."

"Bring a stretcher. He's in no condition to walk"

"Look at all those cuts. We'd better get him to the hospital."

"Na, let our own in-house 'Doc' sew him up. He used to be a paramedic."

"You mean, Butch? He'll have big scars the way he does it."

"So what. Now he'll know what the real world looks like. His face was too perfect anyway."

"His left arm needs to be set. It looks like it might be broken. We gotta get him to a hospital."

"Leave him alone. Butch can fix that too."

Who's this Butch, guy, I thought to myself. *With a name like Butch, it doesn't sound very comforting.*

When we got to the infirmary I was placed on a table and cleaned up by Butch. He was also an inmate, but right now, being awakened at midnight for this job didn't thrill him much, and the wash job was far from gentle. I found out later that Butch was an advanced medical student — until he got messed up on drugs and was convicted of killing some patients. He was in prison for the rest of his life. He was now called "Doc" in here for events like this.

There was no great care in the suturing of my face, or in setting my left elbow. It was amateur at best. Because there was no real doctor around, there was nothing to kill the pain. Thank goodness I was so numb from the beating I didn't feel the stitching being done. After the sewing up of my wounds, I could feel the stubby ends of the silk threads on my face and legs as I brushed my hands over them. My right eye was swollen half closed by the fight, and now the stitches. My left arm hurt a lot, but I was told it would be set tomorrow. A real doctor would look at it. *No real doctor on duty during the night in a large prison?*

After my first day in prison I wished I were dead. I'd often heard people say that in fun, but now I truly knew what it meant. And it was no joke. I - honestly - wished - I - was - dead. Who cares? Who really cares?

At that moment I was at the brink of giving up. Giving up on everyone — my family, friends and yes, even Gwen. Really, now, really, what's the use? Right now they're all sleeping comfortably in their beds and not thinking of me, their son, friend, or boyfriend. The despair and loneliness was so deep I was sapped of any hope. I had slammed into that bottom I knew was coming. I could fall no farther. *Jesus, Gwen says You know everything. If You do, You see this?*

For the next two days I was kept in the infirmary where meals were brought to me, and I had a real bed to lie on and clean sheets. The white painted metal bed frame and the stark, almost empty room with no curtains on the windows looked like a hospital scene from a 1920s movie. There was no beating going on, and for the most part it was quiet — preciously quiet, and no wild swearing or slamming doors. When I looked into a mirror I didn't know the face I saw. It wasn't the face I'd shaved for years, and it sure wasn't the face others admired and took pictures of.

Both Warden Pitts and Chaplain Derek came to see me. The warden just couldn't help sounding mechanical. But I guess with the level of life he had to work with, it was his style. The chaplain was a lot different. He seemed to care. He was truly sorry for the events and spent extra time with me. Butch had tried to do the best he could for me, and he still seemed genuinely concerned about my eye and elbow, saying, "I really hope things come out okay for you. I wish I coudda done a better job on the stitching, but with only a few tools and no pain killers I did my best. I'd like to work Dog over in here for just ten minutes. He keeps me busy. Oops, not 'sposed to say that."

Butch went so far as to give me something for the pain, and even some sleeping pills so I could finally get some decent sleep. I didn't ask where he got the pills. I didn't think I wanted to know.

I kept wondering if they would put me back in with Dog.

For me, this was the whole world I was living in. I'd already lost track of the days. Butch told me it was Wednesday when I came in here, and today was Saturday. *Wednesday. Wasn't that the night Gwen and her friends had their meetings of Christ on Campus?*

Gwen told me later that she and her friends at the C.O.C. house at Northwestern Illinois Christian College had been praying for me on and off that Wednesday as I'd been transported from the intake facility to Putnam Prison. Throughout the day she tried to envision the trip and what I was going through. She prayed that somehow, and in some way, the Lord would show me that He cared for me. Perhaps I would find a Christian inmate who could help me. But not knowing about this made for one of the darkest hours of my life. Gwen thought of that night's message about Old Testament Joseph's pain of being sold by his brothers into slavery. God turned Joseph's dark night into something good, and Gwen knew something good would come to me.

As far as I was concerned, I had often heard that God works in mysterious ways. I thought that if that's true, I could only wonder what mystery God was working on in me.

Gwen told me later that after the C.O.C. meeting that night, she and Erik had walked along the Stony River at the edge of the campus. They enjoyed each other's company. I guess that in Erik's mind he was always planning and thinking how he could get Gwen's mind off me. As a guy his own age, I don't blame him. Whenever the discussion came up, Erik tried to convince her that there would probably not be much of a life for us in the future – when people learned about my prison background. Gwen admitted to me that she did give the possibility some thought. Demon doubt was still grinding on her, she wrote, even though she had promised her heart to me.

If I knew she was walking along the Stony River with Erik at the same time I was being beaten up, I would have let go of any life I had left in me, and just died there on the floor with my career going down the drain.

Chapter Seventeen

While I was in the infirmary something must have been going on in the front offices, because when the guards came to take me back to the cellblock things were different. John, the guard who put me in with Dog in the first place, told me, "I got orders to put you in with another guy."

There is a God! Maybe someone does care. I suddenly thought, and just as fast I thought, *Can I trust this bunch? It might even be worse.*

The guards led me back to a new cell with no handcuffs. I found out later, in that prison, it was up to the guards' discretion whether to use restraints or not. Knowing what just happened to me a few days ago, there was no threat of escape. We walked through the usual set of doors and same halls back to the cellblock. Most of the guys were in the commons. They suddenly stopped whatever talking or watching TV they were doing and looked at me again. This time with gasping expressions. I didn't get it. They saw me arrive in good shape four days ago, and they were all looking at me again. I looked like a rag doll. *Will people ever stop looking at me like I'm a freak?* As I was led to my new cell with my head down, I heard several curse Dog and vow to make him pay for what he did to me.

I didn't see Dog on my return. Someone told me later he was locked down in his cell for a few days — nothing new to him. It seems some guards thought I'd retaliate and punch him out. That didn't take the thinking of a rocket scientist. Did anyone really think I wanted to open that can of worms again?

John took me to another cell and introduced me to an older gray haired, handsome, and slender man of another race, named Tyrone Williams. At first glance I saw hope. *What a difference — an introduction.*

With a smile and a manly handshake, Williams said, "It isn't much, friend, but welcome to your new home."

Home it was. A braided rug by the side of his bunk, books on a shelf, pictures of people on the wall that I took to be his family — and by Tyrone's bunk a picture of Jesus looking right at me with his hands folded. A Bible and a few other books on the small table offered me some comfort, adding to the welcome.

"Which would you prefer, upper or lower bunk?"

I was blown away. Couldn't believe my ears. A *choice — and an educated voice.* Quickly I said, "Top, if you don't mind."

"Great. I'm getting too old to do all that climbing."

I began to feel at ease, especially when John, the guard, put his hand on my shoulder when he was about to leave. "This will be better for you," He said with a sincere voice. I think I sensed a *little* remorse and an unspoken, "I'm sorry." His cold eyes seemed to soften a bit — just a bit.

"Thanks, John, I heard that." I said, with some effort.

There's something about a prison I learned just then. As cold and harsh as it is, once in a great while a crumb, just a morsel, of compassion sneaks in through a crack for a second or two. But no one would admit it.

As my new cellmate began to talk and we got to know each other, Tyrone told me that it wasn't his job to tell me how to behave or who to associate with. That was up for me to learn. "Just think before you step. We all step in it once in a while, but we survive."

He was right. Over the next few days I learned things just like he said I would. I was yelled at a lot and pushed around. Some inmates liked to talk a lot and some had the attitude of, "Shut up and leave me alone." The round tables in the commons had their own private groups and pecking order, some tighter than others. The fact that everyone knew about the fight on my first night, gave me an "in" that other newcomers never had. They all had advice to give me, apart from those who just looked at my face, hung their heads and turned away. For a while I followed Tyrone around like a shadow, and of course my nickname became, "The Shadow."

In that medium prison we were allowed one razor blade at a time, but had to show it to the guards twice a day. Shaving my face with all the stitches sticking out, and the scars swelling up, was a new and painful experience. When I looked at my face all cut and bleeding after I tried to shave, I told myself to give it a rest. For a few weeks I didn't shave at all, thinking that a beard would cover up the mess. It didn't. Most of the cuts and scars were in places even a beard couldn't cover up. I think Dog knew what he was doing and did it well. Tyrone told me a few days later, "Keep washing your face and don't let the beard and cuts from shaving get infected." *Where did he get that wisdom? Did he really care?*

It didn't take long before some gang members came up to me and made it clear I should join them. "Ya know, kid, you better be in our gang."

"Why should I join your gang?"

"Everybody's in a gang for protection."

"Tyrone's not in a gang."

"Oh, Tyrone, he's a simpleton all by himself. He thinks religion will protect him. You need our protection."

"Protection from what?" I asked.

"Being shoved around and beaten up by others around here."

"Look at my face, take a good look," I said in a heavy voice. "I've already had the beating of my life – and where were you?"

"Locked up, stupid. How *could* we help?"

"So what have you done about it since, to show me you'd be worth joining?" Those words were out of my mouth before I knew it. "I haven't seen you kicking Dog around to prove anything to me."

They looked at each other like a bunch of fish on a string. So while I had them on that line I went on, "I don't want or need your gang or any gang. I've had the best 'orientation' anyone could get. I took the beating without your help. I got the message."

One of the gang said, "The only thing on your pretty face that still looks good is your nose, so if you get that that bent out of shape, don't blame us. We gave you a chance."

"If I get beaten up again, I get beaten up again. How could it be any worse? Forget it." I don't ever remember talking like that to anyone in my life. I guess I was inspired. I didn't know if that was the end of the issue or not, but I never heard another word about it from them or from any other gang.

Chapter Eighteen

To begin with, I didn't tell the folks or Gwen how serious the fight had been. I just said it was a pushing and shoving match in getting acquainted and learning a few things around here. Within the second week I received a short note from Gwen, with a lot of fresh encouragement. She had no idea I was about to give up on her after the fight. I left it at that and never mentioned it to her. It was finals at her college and she was understandably crushed for time.

> "Dearest Hunter, I don't know what to say other than I still love you with all my heart. Something weird happened, because this prison life is just not you. I'll stay by your side."

My heart was lifted high as I read these words, but I still felt guilty about the thought of giving up on her after the beating that first night. The idea of giving up on Gwen clawed at me for a long time. I now knew she would not give up on me.

I learned a lot about "jailhouse etiquette" in that

"house of correction," if both those terms fit here. For example, I learned never to ask, "What you in here for?" like I'd seen in the movies. Regardless of the many conversations with Tyrone, I didn't even ask him why he was in here.

Prisoners would either tell me with, "I was framed" somewhere in the story, or I'd find out by rumor. I learned that Dog was originally in a maximum prison for armed robbery and rape, but some group of do-gooders thought it was in his best interest to be sent here for "rehabilitation." He had a strong craving to fight, so his sentence got longer and longer. No kidding. He was already up to eighty-five more years, which meant no chance of breathing fresh air. So why not fight? What did he have to lose? He was housed and fed for the rest of his life.

Tyrone also told me that Dog's real name was Charlie Sullivan, and his father was a Pentecostal preacher. It didn't take long for me to discover Tyrone was a real live born-again Christian. If given the chance, he'd witness and share his faith with anyone — as slim as that opportunity was. A few years ago Sullivan, Dog, with his hard mouth told Tyrone where he could put his witness. "I had enough of that religious hot air all my life, and it never done me no good. Just leave me alone and call me one of your failures." Tyrone learned quickly what Jesus meant when He said, "Shake the dust off your feet "

It took months for me to even find my place in the pecking order. It was more than simple pecking. It was more like, "Shut up, leave me alone," or being pushed and shoved away. My place was nowhere near the top. No one told me what the order was. I had to learn the rank myself. Sometimes I could see Tyrone snickering off in the distance. I was the new kid on the block, or *in* the block. I had no say on conversation, picking a TV channel, or what table to sit at. It was only because of Tyrone and some other older and softer guys that I had anyone to talk to at all.

Another aspect about this new life of mine was the loss of freedom and modesty. As the single son in the family, I knew and appreciated both. Prison is like two guys with criminal backgrounds, not particularly liking each other in the first place, living in a walk-in closet with a toilet. The whole place never smells good. I didn't think I'd ever get used to sitting on that toilet. It was degrading. I always had the feeling of being watched all the time. A day never went by when I wasn't talked down to by inmates and guards. Prison is a cruel and evil place — the furthest thing one can imagine from a country club or cruise ship. Maybe it *was* close to a ship — a slave ship without the whips.

Shortly after I arrived at Putnam Prison, my folks and Gwen sent letters asking when they could come for a visit. I wished they never would have to see this place — or me in it. But I knew it would be impossible to put them off for five to seven years. I also knew how important my looks were to all of them, and I didn't want them to see me like this. As long as the stitches and swelling were still there, and shaving was a problem, I put them off as long as I could. My right eye never did fully recover, but I can see with it even though it remains half closed. My left elbow also never came back right. There was a little twist in my arm, but I could use it pretty well. What's a few missing teeth among prisoners? No one seemed to care about my tribulations, so I learned to stop complaining. I just accepted all this as a new normal, and the way of life in prison. Some things I would just have to deal with in the future.

I felt myself in a life of failure, constant pain, depression, no self-respect, and helplessness. I had nothing to be proud about. I had to write and tell folks and friends that some of the injuries of the fight were worse than I told them at first and that some sores were not yet fully healed.

Chapter Nineteen

Mom and Dad came for their first visit about six weeks after I got there. My sister, Hannah, was afraid to come, and I encouraged her not to. I told her it was okay, and we'd keep in touch by writing a lot. Visiting at that medium security prison depended a lot on who the inmate was and who the visitors were. Fortunately, I was able to meet the folks in a visitors' lounge, but always with guards watching.

I couldn't wait to see them again, but I was sick at heart and seared with embarrassment at the thought of Mom having to go through those searches to get through the gates. She assured me in a recent letter that she knew about the searches and was ready for them. When the door opened and I saw them take their first step into the room, I could hardly keep standing. Mom looked around the room as if searching for someone. I walked up to her.

"Mom."

She gasped, and without thinking quickly brought her hand over here mouth. She obviously hadn't recognized me among the group of people. Her knees buckled and Dad had to hold her up. I think Dad was in

97

the same shock as she was. A woman guard helped them to a corner table.

We melted into a group hug, quivering and weeping. Other families couldn't help looking surprised, but we had been given the permission for physical contact by the guards. They guessed we could be trusted not to pass drugs or weapons. But it was also a show of shame. The meeting was a scene from a nightmare movie and we were playing the lead roles, a part none of us was prepared for. The other inmates told their families about my past and the beating, and why there was such a bad reception from my parents.

"Mom, just don't look at my face if you don't want to. I'll understand."

Squeezing my arms tightly she rose up on her toes to look me squarely in the face. In a very stern and fast voice I'd never heard from her before, she said, "Hunter Thomas Lowe, you are my child. I'll never turn my face from you." Then she kissed me right on the stitches.

The visit passed through blurry tears, but it was so refreshing and wonderful to my weakened spirit. We talked about Hannah finishing high school and choosing a college.

"Boy, thinking of my little sister growing up without me around must be hard on her. How do kids at school treat her?" I asked.

"It's hard at times, Hunter," Mom said. "But you'd be surprised and proud of the spunk she shows whenever your name or situation comes up. She'll stand up to the dumbest remarks and put anyone in their place."

Dad said, "Gwen and the guys would like to visit too when they can all work out a date."

Gwen was now in nursing school and I was glad to hear she wouldn't have to come all the way alone. Who better to be with than Aaron and Bruce? "Don't let them come yet," I said quickly, "but I sure will be glad to see all three of them when I'm looking better than this. Are the neighbors talking much about this?"

Mom and Dad glanced at each other, then Mom said, "There was a little bad talk at first, but it has quieted down. They're mostly supportive now — they often ask about you in a concerned way.

"Here's a flash," Dad said with a burst of excitement. "We've started going to Gwen's church with her folks. I'm surprised how much we enjoy it and how much we're getting out of it. Your Granny was right all along, son. We should have given more thought to church as a family when you kids were young. We missed out on a lot."

"I'm glad to hear that." I said that without thinking, but it was true. I was beginning to think more and more about the things Gwen spoke to me about her faith. "We learn things too late, don't we? Get this, in this crazy world I live in, little things mean a lot. My new cellmate is a guy named Tyrone Williams. He's a strong Christian, and it's made all the difference to my life around here. Mom, Dad, there's a lot of good news about Jesus, isn't there? You know the Reverend Johnson I told you about from Capital City? He told me when I left there, 'It might be in a strange way, but you'll find out how Christ is working through all this.' Boy, was he ever right. I wonder what's next."

We didn't talk about the fight or how I looked, but Mom and Dad were concerned I was doing okay. As the time for the visit was coming to a close, we all decided that we'd hold our heads up. I knew it wouldn't be like this forever. When this prison time was over, we would pick up our lives again.

Mom was so brave, but I could see her start to quiver at the end of the visit. Dad was as strong as he always was, and we hugged again as they left. That morsel of compassion slipped in again as a kindly woman guard helped the folks to the door. Returning to the smelly and noisy cellblock after a high like that was depressing.

Before I landed in this place, Gwen and I emailed each other a lot. Now without our computers or smart phones, we had to write the old fashioned way with pen and paper. It wasn't so bad. The time spent writing Gwen a letter by hand was like being with her. So in this way I could spend time with Gwen whenever I wanted to. Touching the paper she touched was like touching her. I could keep her letters with me all day long, and read them a dozen times. I could kiss the pages and even enjoy the fragrance of her presence whenever I wished — even on my pillow throughout the night. None of that comes with email or texting!

Chapter Twenty

As time went on, Gwen admitted to me in a letter that in spite of her promise, "I'll never find another guy," she couldn't help enjoying talking and walking around campus with Erik. But only as friends, she assured me. But I constantly thought Erik's Danish good looks and charm, with a little gentle persuasion, could have a way of getting to her lonely vulnerability. Their walks around campus, walks by the Stony River, okay. Holding hands, maybe. Embrace or kiss? Never! But did Gwen know these limits?

One especially cool October evening after another meeting of Christ on Campus, while I would have been watching some lame TV program in this dump, Gwen wrote to say that she and Erik were standing at the railing overlooking the Stony River in the light of a full moon. The bright light from the clear moon glistened and seemed to wink at them in the water as it tumbled and twisted its way over the stones in the riverbed. The gentle sound of the splashing water was mesmerizing. She said the conversation went from nowhere to nothing, as simple talk usually does. Erik cupped her little cold hands completely in his large warm hands. He put his arm around her and drew her close to himself against the chill. And for the first time she let him.

Gwen wrote that Erik turned towards her, looking down into her eyes, and she looked back. He lowered his head and kissed her. The kiss was warm and direct. Gwen told me that, without warning, fireworks and explosions erupted in her heart and she pushed him back firmly saying, "*No, no, no!* Oh Erik, this can't be."

"But Gwen..."

"You know how I feel about Hunter. I'm sorry, Erik. I mean it. I'm sorry I led you on."

Surprised, yet sounding as though he was expecting defeat would come sometime, she wrote that Erik said, "You haven't led me on, Gwen. I'm the one who's been doing the leading. As a Christian myself and knowing how you feel about Hunter, I really have been out of bounds. Come on, I'll walk you back to your dorm."

They walked in silence. Gwen told me she was sure she'd done the right thing, and she could tell that Erik now realized any future with her was over. Truly, Gwen's heart was in prison with me. A strange thought, but comforting to me was that Erik realized his role as a Christian and was man enough to live up to it. Could I place him as a friend like Aaron and Bruce?

Life in prison could easily have scarred my mind as badly as my face. I had to work hard on controlling my thoughts every moment of the day and night. I had to keep my mind on the fact that five to seven years *will* come to an end some day in the future, although it seems a long time off right now. I knew I could easily fall into deep depression like so many prisoners do. Depression is an easy place to go to, with nothing but cold walls and bars everywhere. The paint was always chipping off the old bars, and the hinges were rusty. Every door had its own squeak and its own clank. The electronic buzzer on each door had its own tone. I soon began to know which door was opening or closing without looking up. No carpet, no drapes, no pleasant pictures on the walls or any warm touch. Even outside in the prison yard, the walls and tall chain linked fence with rolls of razor wire on top, kept saying, "You're not getting out of here — Hunter Lowe."

Learning the time of guard changes, I even came to know who was coming through the doors. All this ganged up on me and stifled my visions, hopes, and dreams. No wonder lives deteriorate in these cages. Walls and bars place a limit on every scene, idea, and thought I had. No space, no sky, no grass, no hills. Not even a pile of dirt. I tried to figure out why those things meant so much to me, and I discovered it was because I just could not have them in my life now. The only difference between this place and hell is that it was clean here, constant sweeping and brushing kept it like that.

I could only escape the walls within my own mind. For seconds or for hours I could be "outside the quadrilateral parallelogram." Funny why I remembered that geometric term for box from high school, I remember the very day and hour, third hour. It was a

Tuesday that Mr. Vandemark told us. He had a very happy way of teaching math to students. It paid off for me. I could be with my own thoughts — but when reality returned it slammed back with a vengeance. The empty hours and days could have driven me crazy if I hadn't kept my mind working on something. Writing letters did that for me. I even considered writing a book someday.

Chapter Twenty-One

Incredible as it may seem, it was about a full torturous year after I was in prison that Gwen and the guys could work out a time when they could all come for their visit. I looked forward to it with great hope, but also with the fear of what they would have to go through to see me. Our four years in high school were so idyllic and free compared to this human septic tank. I wondered if they had any idea of the harsh conditions they were about to witness.

They were waiting in the lounge that day when I was brought in. Mom had warned them about my appearance, but there was still a second of hesitation and deep breaths when we first saw each other almost a year after the beating. Quickly, the four of us flew into an unashamed hug. There was always a lot of hugging going on, but with only moments to be with someone I cared for, hugging is what I did unashamedly. The friendship of those two guys, Gwen, and me was solid, clean, pure, and beautiful.

Bruce, the tall, skinny one had finally put on some "beef" and filled out, looking good, but no longer usable by Rockwell. Aaron had gotten chunkier yet. Gwen was her true beautiful self, a head turner, a real honest picture of a rose among thorns. Knowing how fast time flies when friends are having a good time, we talked hard and fast about colleges, girlfriends, old friends, and the town. They brought up news about our fifth year high school reunion coming up in a few weeks, and I told them not to be afraid to talk about me. I said I hoped to be at the tenth, and I'd straighten them all out then.

Near the end of the visit, open and blunt Bruce kicked Aaron under the table and said, "Time for us two to go." After handshakes and hugs with promises to keep in touch, they went to the door and asked the guard if they could go to the car.

"No! All three of you came in together and have to leave this building together." He pointed to the door. "But you two can wait down the hall by the steps."

Gwen and I were alone for the remaining minutes of the visit. No one else was in the lounge, except the one guard. I held Gwen's hands and my heart started to beat faster.

I glanced at the guard expecting him to yell at me, but he winked and whispered. "This could cost me my job, but I'll give you kids thirty seconds over there by the green table. Cameras can't see that corner."

Then he did something a prison guard should never do. He turned his back on us. If heaven ever touched earth, it did for thirty seconds that day. I swept Gwen up in an embrace so deep my blood turned warm and every moment of my life was complete. For thirty seconds I was lifted out of that prison into drifting clouds. I felt our hearts pounding with one beat that confirmed to me that our two lives would be one after all this was over.

With a heart full of hope and eyes beyond tears, I said, "Gwen, I can now see that Jesus is somewhere in this mess, and I'm going to find out where."

She burst into tears. "I'm glad to hear that, but Hunter…" Her hands slid from around my neck, down my back and arms, and we locked fingers for a brief moment. "I have to go now," she said quickly.

We hugged for a few more seconds and she ran to the door. It was my feeling she'd just had enough of being in this place. I didn't blame her. Prison has a way of making people want to find the nearest exit, fast.

As she disappeared through the door I finally knew again this prison sentence would one day be just a bad memory. All I had to do was to keep my head straight in this crooked place.

Another guard entered the room, looked at Gwen as she was leaving, and said to me, "You let two guys bring her all the way down here from Ravenswood, alone? You crazy?"

Smiling, and with new found confidence, I proudly informed him, "We've all known each other since we were kicking slats out of our cribs and playing in the sandbox. I'd trust those guys with her for a weekend without a shred of doubt."

He shook his head in disbelief. I took a long look at the other guard. Nothing was said between us, but a great "thank you" from me traveled across the room — that morsel of compassion again.

Soon after Gwen's visit I was given a job in the prison kitchen. Every other day I was secured with the other inmates in the kitchen where we prepared food for about a thousand "clients." We worked on a revolving schedule for two days on and two days off. I found it satisfying that we worked well with each other, but the guards were always counting knives and other tools every half hour. Entrees, vegetables, salads, and desserts were interestingly put together so they could be served on a fast moving chow line. We also set up trays to go to certain "guests" in their own cells, like Charlie Sullivan who was still known as Dog, the one who beat me up that first night.

Within a couple of days of starting in the kitchen, I noticed turkey meat was everywhere. It was in salads, hotdogs, baloney, bacon, cold cuts, turkey-a-la-king, and of course turkey as a main course. I asked the supervisor one day, "Why so much turkey?"

"Think about it, Lowe. It's healthy, easy to fix, plentiful, good for ya, and has that enzyme in it that keeps a guy sleepy. But the biggest reason that turkey is king around here is because it's cheap. The governor likes that reason the best." That mouthful answered any questions I had about the turkey issue.

Time went faster now, with something worthwhile and constructive to do. Cleaning pots and pans even felt good — like washing police cars back in the sally port at the county jail in Capital City. Boy, it's funny how simple and mundane duties become a relief.

What a mixture of mankind in that place. Some talked all the time and some were silent. Some were clean and some didn't appreciate showers. Some found something funny in everything that was said, and some held bitter grudges and cursed all the time. The mix of all types of music and talk shows from radios was always like sandpaper grinding in my ears. There was never any peace and quiet. Future plans were always on the lips of some, while others were just resigned to spending the rest of their lives straining their visions and thoughts through bars. Many used the gym a lot while others let their bodies waste away. When we couldn't get to the gym, bars and pipes in our cells worked just as well for pulling and lifting exercises.

There was also the group that found life in prison easier to live because there were no decisions to make. They found it a warm place to spend the winters. They knew just what crimes to pull off to win a four to six month retreat from cold weather. One guy told me, "Beats spending the cold night behind a dumpster."

The characters that made up the population of the cell block looked like they came from a movie casting company. Two that stood out were ones they called Tweedledum and Tweedledee, two rather short stocky guys who were always together when out of their cells. They made up the comedy team of the house. If they didn't wear separate clothes you'd think they were joined at the hip. Their humor was well laced with the standard prison vocabulary.

I never got to the point of trusting anyone other than Tyrone. I was glad to be in his cell. He had an unshakable faith in God that stood above the demeanor and attitudes of all the rest. There was nothing phony about his faith or words. Some other guys would talk Jesus words, but Tyrone and some of us could see right through their thin and empty theology. Their conversation meant nothing. The other guys wouldn't talk much religion, but Tyrone was deeply respected by everyone in that place, even by the guards. I could feel that respect just by being around him all the time. As to why he was in prison — not a clue. He never wanted to talk about why he was there. The only thing I knew about his sentence was that it was for life without parole. And I wondered how he could stay sane with that hanging over his head. But I could see it was his love for God, and God's love for him, that kept him going.

As the months ran into years, I kept as busy as I could writing letters to friends and even strangers. I also found I could write letters for other inmates who could not write. People who could not write today? I found them there. I also found an occasional inmate who could carry on a good sensible and educated conversation without cursing and bitter rancor. Working in the kitchen was a big help, but the best time I had — if there was such a thing — was getting on the prison baseball team. High school and college teams would come to the prison for games. The games brought back a lot of good memories of high school with Aaron and Bruce. But of course we only had home games, no road trips.

Chapter Twenty-Two

Just when I thought I'd seen and heard every color, flavor, fragrance, and species of mankind in this collection, one Tuesday afternoon I met another. Actually I heard him before I saw him. All the heads in the commons suddenly looked towards the entrance door as we heard yelling and scuffling like none of us had known before. And in a prison, that's saying something. The opening buzzer of that door was quickly followed by more yelling and the most debauched language even the hardest in our "neighborhood" ever heard.

The little guy making all the noise was nothing more than a wobbling bowling pin being pulled, dragged, and pushed into the commons by at least four guards, each twice his size. He was handcuffed and shackled, with chains connecting them. We saw the tightest of security measures for that place suddenly come up. Whatever this new "client" was trying to prove, was not being taken lightly by John and his personal swat team. They half dragged, half pushed this little squirming guy down the polished floor. Warden Pitts followed this traveling dog fight with a trace of a smile on his face. We all froze in our tracks or conversations as we watched this skirmish play out right in front of us.

This little pudgy man, about four feet tall, two hundred pounds, with clothes that fit him like a clown, was making each one of those guards earn their pay that day. The bald head had less than a dozen wild hairs, and his ears stuck out like Dumbo's. He was missing a few assorted teeth, and his eyes were bugged out like someone was standing on the back of his neck. None of us had ever heard the way he eloquently crafted Satan's Dictionary. Within minutes that day, new number 576110 showed the most seasoned veteran of the art of swearing a new dialect. It was enough to make a prison guard or sailor blush. He taught us new verbs and nouns for feet, doors, floors, and faces. I knew what it was like to have an eye sewed up: I wondered if Butch could sew up his mouth.

It was obvious they were heading towards the "orientation cell," expecting Dog to do his job. "Don't bring that blob in here. I don't want him," Dog yelled.

John yelled right back, "Charlie, you're the only one that can break him."

"Look at him, I can't improve on that. The world beat him up better than I can. Besides, I done beating on people. I done enough of your dirty work. I don't beat up new guys no more. Throw him someplace else. I'm tired." Charlie was right, that little mass of a man *had* been beaten up — and down — by the lineup of DNA.

Because it was late in the afternoon when 576110 was brought in, and the guard's shift was almost done for the day, they pushed him into a rare empty cell for the rest of the night.

"Don't get too used to this," John said. "It's just for tonight."

After about a half hour of solitary mumbling, swearing, and yelling, 576110 wound down. He was left in his cell for dinner. Another tray of turkey cold cuts served. I'm sure the rest of the guys thought the same thing I did: would he be put in with any of us?

I discovered the complete mix of religions makes for a strange stew in prisons. Muslims, Jews and all branches of Christianity from Catholics to Pentecostals try to live in the same line of cages. Even the atheists and agnostics expressed their strong beliefs if they could find a leg to stand on. There was nothing comfortable or dependable with this bunch when it came to talking about what they believed. A lot of bitterness, shame, ignorance, and hostility showed up in the occasional argument about religion. Strange and empty doctrinal teachings showed their hollowness. Arguing about politics was almost never heard. No one really knew what was going on outside anyhow. I found it best to stay away from any conversation on the subjects, because they usually turned into arguments. I wasn't too sure of my own views anyway. Surprisingly, we all got along without cracking skulls.

Although religious discussions were dangerous at times, there were often religious services down in the little theater on a lower level. Those who didn't like to go to them just stayed in their cells or the commons. Certain times of the year visiting clergy of all faiths would come and minister to the assorted "congregations." It was something different to do for a while, and I suppose there was some meaning to them. If nothing else, for the memories each brought from their childhood or better times.

One usual visitor we could count on was Reverend Crowley, the fisherman, as he liked to be called. He was slight and wiry of build, ruddy in his face with deep-set lines around the eyes and chin. He was always full of enthusiasm and he enjoyed talking to absolutely anyone regardless of their faith. He was from the nearby town, came faithfully every other Sunday afternoon, and held an old-fashioned church service in that little theater.

We'd sing a few simple songs while Sammy Gold, a skinny guy with no chin who looked more like another Norman Rockwell character rather than a prisoner, played an old out-of-date and out-of-tune upright piano that some departed saint donated to the state. To add to this mix, he was of Jewish background, so playing Christian songs and hymns with a happy Hebrew beat was a new experience for him.

Reverend Crowley would share some event from the outside that would be appropriate, have a testimony or two either from a visitor or an inmate, and a prayer and a short message. Knowing the attention span of this congregation, his messages were about seven minutes long. It was a struggle to preach to that crowd, but he was faithful to the very few Christian inmates who appreciated and depended on him.

Dog would come to the theater for these visits once in a while, and always sit in one particular windowsill. Guards would constantly try and get him to sit in one of the chairs, but he'd just glare at them until they sulked away. Dog was the true example of an inmate running the institution with a glare, grunt, and a threat. He never sang at all. He just sat there. When he wanted to leave, he'd grumble something to the guards about hearing all this stuff before. "I'm goin' home." Being the rebellious son of a Pentecostal pastor, I think he was drawn to the services in some way, yet he couldn't handle it once they started. So he demanded a guard or two take him back to the cellblock.

Tweedledum and Tweedledee would also come to the services just to get out of the cellblock for a while, but would do their usual snickering and laughing at the visitor. Pastor Crowley, bless his heart, would put up with it, but sometimes would really put them in their place with a sharp remark about not being funny. He had a unique way of sinking that two-edged sword into them. Number 576110 came the first Sunday he was there, but the guards had to remove him because of the competition he dished out to the preacher. In a few days I was to be surprised in a new way.

Chapter Twenty-Three

About two and a half years after I was incarcerated — that's a nice word for being put in jail — I received a special letter from Pastor Johnson of the City Center Church in Capital City. He had been writing regularly like he promised, but this letter had a sentence it in that almost made me choke. He wrote that he and Ben Marshall would like to come and visit me. *Visit me?* I'd killed Ben Marshall's wife in the accident that got me here in the first place. I couldn't imagine why Ben Marshall would want to see me. I messed up his life big time. So other than making me feel worse, what was the point of a visit from him? The fact that Reverend Johnson would be with him gave me some comfort, so I agreed to the visit — reluctantly.

The day for the visit arrived, and when I was brought into the lounge they both stood up and we all shook hands. As I slowly reached for Ben Marshall's hand, a flood of miserable memories flashed over me as fast as the crash itself. I broke down. Mr. Marshall grasped my right hand and with a firm grip put the other arm on my right shoulder. I thought I'd composed myself after the years, but I just wept like a baby and could only talk through quivering lips and choked emotions, but I managed to get out, "I'm sorry, I'm so sorry, so sorry, Mr. Marshall, I'm so sorry."

He put his right hand on my other shoulder and looking me right in the eyes said, "The reason I'm here, Hunter, is to tell you that God has led me to forgive you. Christ forgave me of my sins, and as a Christian I want you to experience that same forgiveness from me."

I heard the words he spoke, but I didn't understand them. I never heard of such a thing: forgiving someone for killing a loved one?

We didn't move from where we were standing. "Hunter, I can't say this was an easy decision to make or this is easy to say, but Jesus and I go back a long way. I really do forgive you. I want you to know God's grace, and if Jill was here I'm sure she would forgive you too. To be honest, the kids, Marc and Kristin didn't want me to come here today. They're ten and eleven now. They still have a hard time with this, but they both assure me they're working on it. They too know Christ as their Savior."

Coupled with a unique relief in my heart after all those years, there was an unusual feeling of a deep affection for this guy. Our lives had been brought together in an ugly instant as a result of my ignorance and stupidity over that drinking thing. Now I felt I was in the presence of an older brother I never had. I started to see a new reason to find out more about this Jesus whom some people talked about like a friend.

The visit went on for the usual half hour, and we talked about Ben's kids and how the congregation of City Center Church was supporting them. I also learned that the congregation of his church was praying for me. Praying for *me*! That really blew my mind. Why should they do that for me — someone they never knew? It was a remarkable story and all too soon the guard came forward. This time he talked in a different tone, using my name. "Hunter, I'm sorry, the time is up." That morsel of compassion had leaked in for a moment.

Ben assured me one last time he honestly meant what he said. "I forgive you." He made me promise that I would visit him and the kids when I was released. When we shook hands again, I said, "I can't thank you enough for your visit and forgiveness, but I don't know if I could face your kids."

"In time, I know they will want to forgive you also."

I shook my head in disbelief. As they stepped out the door, I realized two gigantic men had put a permanent stamp on my life. While I stood there waiting for a guard to open the door to the cellblock, I thought to myself, *I've got to find out more about this Jesus.*

I walked back to the cellblock, and the emotion of the visit showing in my eyes must have made me look like a raccoon — with one of them half-closed of course. Everyone stared at me again. Would it ever stop? Dum and Dee stopped their laughing for a second; then started to laugh at me. 576110 just sat there not knowing what to do or even say. No words of his eloquent vocabulary drifted from him.

I got to the cell and thank goodness, Tyrone was there. I grabbed his hand and said, "Mr. Marshall forgave me for the accident and what happened to his family. How could he do that?"

"He loves the Lord. He's following the words and commands of Jesus. Don't you get it yet?"

"Okay, roomie, tell me all about your Jesus."

Chapter Twenty-Four

Like a teacher starting a class, Tyrone sat down on the lower bunk. "Hunter, sit down and get ready for the ride of your life. Let's establish a couple of facts first. Do you believe in God, and that the Bible is His Word?"

"Yeah, I do."

"Good, then God has a wonderful plan for your life, and He wants to complete it in you."

Slapping the cold block wall, I had to ask, "And all *this* is part of God's plan for my life? This place, loss of my looks, job, money, the beating, the pain and anguish of my family and friends? Killing Mrs. Marshall? Not a very smart plan, if you ask me."

In a quiet and steady voice Tyrone continued, "You'll see. And best of all, you'll understand it."

I shook my head. "Don't stop now. This ought to be good."

He picked up his Bible, always at hand, and opened it to a page just like he knew where it was, handed it to me and said, "It all starts right here. Read this verse." He pointed to John 3:16. "For God so loved the world that he gave his one and only Son, that whoever believes in him shall not perish but have eternal life." Then to John 10:10. "The thief comes only to steal and kill and destroy; I have come that they may have life, and have it to the full."

"If God loves the world and all of us in it," I said, "and if He wants us to have a great life, why doesn't everybody have it? He could do that, couldn't He?"

Tyrone smiled in understanding. "You couldn't have asked a better question. I knew you'd say that. You see, when God made man He didn't make a robot, or another object of creation. God created man with a free choice. Look at the crowd in this place, and a lot of other people you know. They choose not to love God. That makes a great separation, sort of a huge pit between a Holy God and sinful man."

Giving that a minute to sink in, I said, "Then I guess I have to find a way to get across that pit, huh?"

Nodding his head and smiling, he just kept going on without a glitch. "You catch on fast. Man has been trying to do that throughout the ages of all human existence. Read these two verses now: Romans 3:23 and Romans 6:23. 'For all have sinned and fall short of the glory of God.' And, 'For the wages of sin is death, but the gift of God is eternal life in Christ Jesus our Lord.'

"Man has tried all kinds of good works." Tyrone continued. "All kinds of religions, sacrifices, fancy philosophies, all types of highly educational pursuits, morality, and even technology. But nothing man can do will bridge that pit. It's like building a bunch of bridges that don't reach the other side. Now here's where God

121

comes into our lives. He bridged the pit with His own sacrifice, the death of His own Son, Jesus. If you can grip this next thought you'll know how great God really is. Jesus, who is God in the flesh, laid down His life for us. That means Christ died for *you,* Hunter Lowe. He is the sacrifice for our sins, yours and mine, not the other way around like other religions want it. God does the work, God is the sacrifice. Look at these two verses from Ephesians 2:8-9.

"'For it is by grace you have been saved, through faith – and this not from yourselves, it is the gift of God – not by works, so that no one can boast.'

"Hunt, Jesus Christ is the answer to this problem of separation and sin. You, me, everybody, good or bad, rich or poor, good looking or ugly, all need to go through Jesus to get to that holy God. Jesus is that bridge."

He pointed out two more verses to me. Romans 5:8. 'But God demonstrates his own love for us in this: While we were still sinners, Christ died for us.' And in John 14:6. 'Jesus answered, I am the way and the truth and the life. No one comes to the Father except through me.'

"It's through His grace and His forgiveness that we're saved, Hunt, that's all there is to it."

"Like what Marshall did for me?" I blurted out.

"Better than that, my friend. Marshall forgave you for the accident and the death of his wife. Jesus will forgive you for *all* your sins."

"Hang on now, Ty, I've been a good kid all my life. I didn't smoke, drink – not until *that* night. I didn't do drugs, or use God's name in swearing. I loved my folks, respected Gwen more than I wanted to at times, and did other good stuff. Do I still need to be saved?"

Tyrone took a deep breath, but he didn't sound annoyed. "A minute ago I said, 'You catch on fast.' Now I'm wondering. Don't you remember what you just read in Romans 3:23? 'All have sinned and come short of God's glory.' See, Hunt, John 12:6 says that God has provided the only way. You have to make the choice. Your girlfriend Gwen made the choice. Reverend Johnson did at one time. Even Ben Marshall and his kids made the same choice. Look what their lives have done for you. Can you see how Jesus is working because He cares for you?"

From just outside the cell, Dum and Dee were sitting at one of the tables in the commons. Dee said, "Sounds like Deacon Williams is turning up the heat on Lowe."

Dumb answered with, "Yeah, we ought to hear the 'Come on down to the front next.'"

From farther down the row of cells, 576110 yelled, "What kind of talk is that?" but without any of his multicolored words.

Chuckling, Tyrone said, "Don't listen to 'em. It's just Satan using a bunch of his own crowd to interfere with God's plan."

I said, "Ty, there's a lot here to think about. I'd like to talk about this with the preacher when he comes next week."

"That's great. Read one more verse. This in time from the book of Revelation, chapter three, verse twenty."

He pointed to the verse and I read it aloud. "Here I

am! I stand at the door and knock. If anyone hears my voice and opens the door, I will come in and eat with him, and he with me."

"That's Jesus talking straight to you, friend. He's knocking at the door of your heart — and your brain. Don't wait too long."

In the nine days before Reverend Crowley returned for his usual service, Tyrone and I talked a lot about these verses. I told him they were making a lot of sense to me, but I was still trying to figure out why God would care about a beaten-up guy like me. I asked him one morning, "With my face looking like a road map, can God use me now?"

"Believe me, Hunter, I don't understand it, but if God saves you, He'll use you. He can use you, me, and everyone else in this and other prisons. Even Charlie and his ilk. You haven't forgotten Charlie the dog, have you? Your first night here?"

Without blinking or setting his razor down, he pointed at me with the razor. "God wanted to use you before you got beaten up. What you look like now doesn't matter to Him at all. He still has a plan for you and I think it's going to be great."

"How come you know so much about all this stuff? You've been in here for a long time and will never get out for some reason you don't talk about. Where did you learn all about this salvation and what you so strongly believe?"

"I know this 'stuff,' as you call it because what else is

there to do in this gated community? I read the Bible, other Christian books, study, and pray a lot. It also keeps my brain off of what I'm in here for." Knowing what I was about to ask, "Don't go there!"

"Okay, but you know as much as a preacher does."

"Hunt, when I was a little kid, my granny made sure I got on a blue church bus from one of those Bus'n Baptist churches."

"I had a grandma like that too. Only she took my sister and ..."

Tyrone cut me off. "You asked, and as I was saying, Granny dragged me to that Sunday school and I don't even remember the name of the church. Doesn't matter anyway. They were good at what they did to little minds. Things stuck in our heads. They never let up on the message of forgiveness and salvation. We got kind of bored of it, but now I can see what they were doing. They were planting the seeds of God's Word deep in our hearts and heads."

"You remember all that after what you did, whatever that was?"

"Thanks to the preacher, when I got pulled out of the jaws of Satan, the Holy Spirit brought all those stories and little songs of Sunday school back to me, and I found that perfect peace Paul talks about in his letters."

"Peace, even in *here*?"

"Right, in here. One more thing. When I was in Junior high and just before I jumped ship from Sunday school, they started to teach us the Apostles' Creed."

"O yeah, that statement of, 'I believe in God the

Father ...'"

"That's the one. Years later when I opened the door of my heart to Jesus, I remembered that creed we had memorized. In that statement is everything a Christian should know about what they believe. When I'm asked, 'What do you believe?' it's in there. All the facts. If someone wants to argue, that's their problem. Take it or leave it, that's it for me."

Chapter Twenty-Five

One day, Tweedledum and Tweedledee took it upon themselves to chew on the new meat and find out what 576110's name really was. So they squeezed him between their stubby bodies at a table in the commons. I was at a nearby table and watched their effort at a counseling session. They attempted to talk to him, only to be dusted and cursed at in return.

"Shut up, shrimp. Don't you know how to just talk to someone?" Tweedledum answered. "Now what's your name?"

"It ain't Shut up, and it ain't Shrimp." Pointing to his full number, "It's five, seven, six, one, one, zero to you, Nit."

Looking around in front of 576110, Tweedledee said to Tweedledum, "Now ain't he the cute one? Smart guy too."

Tyrone came by just then and tried his tender approach to the conversation with 576110. "Hi, I'm Tyrone Williams. Welcome to our little corner of the world. Ever been in a prison before?"

"Well, who in Jerusalem are you? The chaplain? I

been in six joints. This dump is number seven, and maybe more to come. So what?"

Tyrone tried again in his cool way to break his shell. "We all go by names in here. It makes things a little bit more pleasant."

"Pleasant, schmellant, I'm 576110 to those jerks, and 576110 to you too. What part of that don't all you airheads understand?"

Tyrone had met his match. "Hunter, why don't you give it a try and talk to him?"

"Yea, tall one, why don't you try and talk to me? Sheee, look at all them scars. Who clawed your face?"

"The best." I said. "You're lucky he refused to work you over."

"That gorilla down there?"

"Yep. And he did it all in a few minutes. On my first night here."

Talking about the beating must have softened 576110 a little, just a little, because he actually let up on his vile defense. He even seemed interested. "No kidding. He done all that to you and you don't get back at him? Your body looks like you could. What kind of a man are you?"

"Hopefully one who doesn't want the fight to keep going."

"Ya got a point there, I guess."

Noticing a slight decrease in the verbal fight, Tweedledum said, "We don't mean no harm. What's your name?"

"I think I see that, but don't laugh."

Standing back a little. *How bad could it be?* I

thought.

"It's Wilts. Seymour Wilts."

Blessed silence prevailed as eight eyeballs flashed in all direction, but had a short lifespan of seven seconds. Tyrone turned his head and Tweedledum and Tweedledee couldn't control themselves. They doubled up laughing and almost fell off the benches. "Seymour Wilts? That's funny. The name don't even stand up by itself," Tweedledum blurted out laughing at the same time as Tweedledee dropped his head onto the table banging his hand in excitement.

"Okay, you jerks, you said you wouldn't laugh, but there ya go, just like everybody I ever try to talk with. See why I hide behind my mouth? How'd you like the nickname, 'Number eight'?"

"Number eight? Why Number eight?" I asked.

When he stood up, and we didn't even notice that he did, he said with a spiteful expression, "Just look at me. Short, fat, bald, big ears, big fat nose, eyes bugging out, and I waddle when I walk. Who do you think that looks like?"

Blank looks and shrugged shoulders hung out all around the table.

"Long time ago someone made a movie about my seven brothers. They all worked in a diamond mine and had some white chick keep their house in the forest clean. You figure it out. You're the smart ones. Now you see?" He turned away and walked — waddled — to his cell.

Tweedledee turned to us and said quietly, while

chuckling, "He does look like that bunch, don't he?"

Tyrone added, "The little guy has a soft button after all."

Chapter Twenty-Six

The following Sunday, the service in the theater went as usual, with the same usual songs *Amazing Grace* and *The Old Rugged Cross* from wrinkled handouts. Funny thing about those handouts, the preacher would never get them all back, yet there were never any left lying around on the floor at the end of the service. The preacher introduced a visitor that day. He called him a "Dramatic Baritone," and he had a guitar with him.

O great, I thought. *A singer. Just what we need around here! A guy to sing a song. What's this going to be, a man version of Maria from Sound Of Music?*

Gabe Jackson, aka, "Chunks," was a 325-pound gigantic black offensive lineman from the N.F.L. whom I'm sure we all recognized. When he smiled and started to speak, all 325 pounds went into action. "The one point I want to make clear to you guys," he said, while pointing his fingers at us, "is that all this Jesus stuff you've heard isn't just for grannies and little girls. All the hotheaded punks you know aren't afraid to tell you what they think about anything, are they? Well, you all know about my sinful past from news stories and magazines, but I don't

131

care what others think of me now. This tough old bird is here to tell ya that I love Jesus — and I'm not afraid to say so. My whole message is about Jesus, so stay put and I'll prove it to ya.

Gabe Jackson set his haunches on a high stool and went right into a short story. "At another prison I was visiting last week, a maximum joint, a smart-head heroically informed me, 'All that Jesus stuff ain't for me. I'm a man, I got hair on my chest,' I ripped my shirt open, blowing buttons all over the place, and said, 'What do you think I got — feathers?'"

I rolled my eyes to get a quick look at Wilts and noticed his mouth was hanging opened like a dead man as he watched and listened, but he didn't move a muscle. Gabe struck a strong chord on his guitar and in a heavy, deep, unashamed, resonating voice sang a song that I had never heard before: *No One Ever Cared for Me Like Jesus*.

As he started to sing, I don't know what the others were thinking, but my mind seemed to soak in everything I heard.

The song was about an experience Gabe had. It was about him finding a new friend who was stronger and more honest than any others he had ever known. This friend was Jesus, and He did something for Gabe no one else could do. Part of the song was about Gabe's old life that was full of sin when this new friend found him. In fact his life was full of misery and despair. *I certainly knew what that was like.* Then Gabe said Jesus put His arms on him and showed him the real way to life.

Some of the guys started to squirm in their seats, but Gabe kept on singing in the same tough surefooted way he drove through a defensive line. He continued that Jesus comes to him every day with more assurance and promises, and now he understands the words of Jesus. He sang he'll never know why Jesus saved him – but some day when he sees Jesus face to face he can ask Him.

In a chorus that came between each verse, half singing and half talking, it sounded like the most honest thing I'd ever heard. Gabe said Jesus is the only one who ever really cared for him. He's never known a friend as kind as Jesus. No one else could have lifted him from all the darkness and filth he lived in. Jesus really *did* care for him.

Every time Gabe sang the chorus it spoke deeper and deeper to me. Walking around the room, strumming the guitar and singing, gave him the opportunity to tap some guys on the shoulders and look right into the eyes of others. At one time he bent over and almost got into Wilts' face. Wilts leaned back and swung his feet, although they didn't reach the floor. Gabe was so into what he was singing, he wiped sweat from his brow and tears from his eyes with a towel slung around his neck glistening with sweat.

Gabe played the guitar with the same gusto he sang. He used strong heavy Spanish type playing with rich, deep chords that added muscle to his singing. The words of that new song were the words I wanted to hear ever since the night of the accident. They drove right into my bones. I finally discovered that someone *does* care for me. Gabe went on and talked about Jesus like he was a friend, then sang a song I remembered from the little Baptist church years ago, *What A Friend We Have In Jesus.*

After a few more words about this Friend of his, Gabe sang another song I'd never heard. He said the name of the song was, *I'd Rather Have Jesus.*

When he started to sing this one I wondered where he was going. He was singing that he'd rather have Jesus. *Rather than what? Who?* He was singing about silver, gold, other riches, and a lot of property. Gabe's a wealthy N.F.L. player with about everything a guy could want, but he'd rather be led my Jesus' nailed pierced hand. I guess the nail holes in Jesus' hand meant a lot to him.

This man singing to us was not only rich but he was famous too. He went on to sing that He'd rather have Jesus than all the cheering and applause of the crowd in a stadium. He'd rather know Jesus than have all the fame in the world. He just wanted to be true and honest to Jesus. I had a hard time getting my head around those words. I'd never heard about Jesus in that way — and this from a guy like Gabe Jackson to whom everything was all about Jesus.

This big bellowing giant of a tough guy, who knew both riches and fame, would settle for just having Jesus. Gabe was singing all this in a prison among some of the meanest people I'd ever known, and this was just a medium security prison. He wasn't a bit ashamed or intimidated. He went on and said that all his hungering spirit needed was Jesus. He'd rather have Jesus lead him, than the best coach in the league.

When Gabe sang that he'd rather have Jesus than anything in the world, this guy got to me. His thinking and life was settled on a bedrock foundation and he knew it. That's what I wanted.

Like the other songs, Gabe sang it with such conviction I couldn't move. Coming from this big sweating and heavy man with the force of a hammer on an anvil, the words grabbed my ears and pinned 'em back.

Between his words and songs, it was as if he was speaking straight to me. As he closed the service he said, "Guys, sing this next song with me. You don't need your song sheets for this one."

He started to sing the song I heard long ago, *Jesus Loves Me*. Little by little we all started to sing that simple chorus and when it was over no one looked around. I don't think anyone wanted to be seen with moist eyes. I never heard it so quiet in that place.

Dog stayed for the whole service that day, but he was the first to leave. Gabe Jackson's commanding presence and thundering voice nailed me to the chair in that theater. I'm sure others felt the same way, because there just wasn't any movement for a while. I couldn't help but think that if Jesus could use a man like Gabe, surely He could use me – somewhere.

After the service, the preacher introduced me to Gabe and he joined us in our discussion over in a corner. Tyrone said, "Hunter and I have been looking at the verses to salvation, he's about ready to give his life to the Lord."

"Yeah, well with one more question," I pushed in there. "I've always lived a good life. You know, did all the right things and didn't sin a lot. Do I really need to be saved?"

The preacher's face lit up like someone gave him a gift. "Hunter, the Bible tells us the story about a good guy, just like you, named Nicodemus who came to Jesus late one night. He asked Jesus the same question you're asking. Jesus told him he would have to be born again, but Nicodemus couldn't understand this 'born again' thing. Jesus cleared it up. A natural birth is natural, but if you want to go to heaven you'll need a spiritual birth."

"Yeah, I guess I do need to be saved. I killed a woman — by accident, though."

The preacher leaned towards me. "Hunter, you needed to be saved long before the accident. Everybody needs to be saved: good guy, bad guy, good looking or ugly."

This was too much for me to handle. "But what use would God have for a guy that killed someone?"

"Let me deal with this one," Gabe demanded. "Kid, have you heard the names Moses, David, and the apostle Paul?"

"Of course I have. What do they have to do with me?"

"All of those guys killed people in violent ways on purpose, yet God used them, didn't He?"

"Hunter," Reverend Crowley broke in, "I know you didn't intend to kill Mrs. Marshall. It was a tragic accident. But no matter how evil a crime, even deliberate murder, don't let guilt stop you from inviting Christ into your heart."

Tyrone added the final touch. "From what I hear about the Marshalls, Jill herself would tell you to accept Jesus and let Him take over your life."

The time was gone again all too fast. The preacher and Gabe had to go. No guests for turkey dinner here. As he was ready to leave, Gabe picked me up like I was a little child, hugged me. He held me at a distance like you would hold a child, looked me right in the eye and said, "Hunter, do what Tyrone did. Build your house, your life, on the Rock — the Rock called Jesus."

Chapter Twenty-Seven

For the next two weeks I must have acted like I was zoned out. My head was so full of good news and hope, yet I couldn't stop wondering why God was leaning so heavy on me. I knew there was something in what He was trying to get through to me. In fact, for a few days I was arguing with God in the warring parts of my brain. *"Why do I need You? I had a good job, money, friends, nice car, girl to marry, and good looks to be a model. I had it all without You."*

"Right, Hunter. You had *all that didn't you? You* had *all that, but you don't have them now, and you didn't have me saving you from hell. What's holding you back, son?"*

I could almost hear Him saying, *"Let go, let go. Let me lead your life from now on. You're not getting anywhere by yourself."* It was as if I could feel the banging of His fist on the door of my heart, yet He wasn't pounding the door down. Not forcing His way in.

I discovered it was useless for me to argue with God. I got to the point where killing Jill Marshall was not the big factor in my thoughts anymore. Ben Marshall's forgiveness, the words of Tyrone, and the preacher had convinced me I was the only one standing in the way of accepting Christ. I was spending too much of my life trying to build those bridges over that pit between God and myself — and failed every time.

Gwen was back at nursing school when I wrote her and told her what I was thinking. She wrote right back saying she was so happy to hear the news. When she opened my letter she said she had cried, laughed, shouted, and danced around the mailroom right there in the student center.

"I couldn't help myself," she wrote. "I must have looked like I was crazy, because others were laughing at me. My prayers for you are now going to be in a different direction."

I wondered what she meant.

A few days later I received a Bible in the mail from Gwen, and on the front page she'd written, "Dearest Hunter, I knew it, I knew it. After knowing you all these years and watching you struggle in that place, I was sure my prayers would be answered and you'd find your way to Christ. That's why I stayed with you. If you accept Jesus now, His promises will fill your life with things you haven't even thought of because Jesus cares for you. Hunter, He always has and always will. Think about Romans 5:8 (look it up). Think about these things too."

At first I thought Gwen had written me a poem, but it was a list of things to think about. She headed it *Because He Cares.*

"Because He cares … your granny took you to Sunday school.

Because He cares, you have great folks and a wonderful sister.

Because He cares, you have two of the best friends a guy could have in Aaron and Bruce.

Because He cares, you could trust Mr. Hall. You had a good career.

Because He cares, you have been a great encouragement to Tyrone.

Because He cares, you have new friends in Pastors Johnson and Crowley.

Because He cares, you have known God's fantastic grace through Ben Marshall.

Because He cares, you are not full of fear these days in that awful place.

Because He cares, you heard Gabe Jackson sing about Jesus just when you needed it most.

Because He cares … I love you.

This list will grow longer and longer in the years to come."

When I put all those things together, I couldn't stop thinking that if I've got all this going for me, what should I be afraid of? In the kitchen I became lost in thought and would accidentally peel too many potatoes, or burn the toast just enough to set off the smoke alarms and send the guards into spasms. I read stories of great Christians from Tyrone's bookshelf. I talked to inmates I'd usually ignore, like Seymour Wilts. Once in a while I even said,

"Hi" to Charlie Sullivan. He still controlled the attitude of fear throughout the prison, but as I began to see how God was working in my life I came to the place where I couldn't call him Dog any longer. No man deserves a title like that – not even Charlie Sullivan. I learned in prison that guys usually live up to the nicknames they're given. Tweedledum and Tweedledee were good examples.

When I lay down on the bunk to go to sleep on clear nights I noticed the moon would try and pry itself through the wires in the small window telling me there was a fresh world out there waiting for me. My mind started to think of all the good things that have been a part of my life in the past. The conversations between Tyrone and myself during the recent weeks were always before me. I thought over and over about the words of how he built his life on Jesus Christ whom he called the Rock.

Then it hit me. The Rock! Tyrone's life! His life was his house! Tyrone had built his house on the Rock!!! The memory of that little Sunday school song came back to me like being hit with a hammer. That's what that song meant – build your life on Jesus. Dah! Why did it take me twenty years to figure that out? My head really was thick. Why was I still stalling?

Another one of those little Sunday school songs came back to me. *I Will Make You Fishers Of Men.* I quickly thought of Reverend Crowley. He called himself, "The fisherman." That was his nickname and that was what he was doing: fishing for men – men to come to Jesus. Now it was starting to make a lot of sense. Those little songs I sang as a child meant a lot more than I ever thought. *Be careful little eyes, what you see, hands what you do, feet where you go ...* I should have been careful not to have walked into *Tommy's Tap* that night six years ago.

Days and days went on, and I thought about nothing but those simple Sunday school songs from that little Baptist church so many years ago. One after another, they just kept coming back to me through the two prisons I was in — one with brick walls and iron bars, the other, an obstinate heart.

The little songs flooded over me: *Heavenly Sunshine; Deep And Wide; Fishers of Men; Stand Up For Jesus; Jesus Loves Me; There's Within My Heart A Melody; Blessed Assurance, Jesus is mine; Jesus, Jesus, Precious Jesus; O How I Love Jesus; Thank You, Lord, For Saving My Soul; I would Be True; Wonderful Grace Of Jesus; I Have The Joy, Joy, Joy, Joy Down In My Heart; Trust And Obey; This Little Light Of Mine; What a Friend We Have In Jesus.* They were all about Jesus. Just the thing a little kid needs to put in his mind and heart to be discovered later.

Echoes of those songs bounced around in my head for days, and I realized how much muscle they have for the storms of my life. I wish Mrs. Gustafson or any of my Sunday school teachers could know how important these songs had become to this guy in prison. I imagined Granny's hand cuffing me on the back of my head. *"Do you get it now, Hunter? That's why I took you to Sunday school."* Twenty-three years later, Granny's efforts paid off.

Chapter Twenty-Eight

During a cool October night, four years after I was sent to prison, all my thinking and waiting came to a sudden end. At 1:30 a.m. I was lying on my upper bunk and not able to sleep. That bright moon was working its way through the thick wire laced glass and Jesus was doing that knocking (banging was a better term) thing at the door of my heart. I recalled another little song from long ago: *Into my heart, into my heart, come into my heart, Lord Jesus; Come in today, come in to stay, come into my heart, Lord Jesus.*

Surrounded in this hard and smelly place of evil men, Jesus zeroed into me. My mind said, *"Yes."* My heart opened. The fight was over. The battle won, and the war was finished. I heard Jesus say from the cross in clear words just for me, *"It is finished, Hunter. I have set you free."*

I finally let Jesus bridge that pit, step into my sinful heart and clean it up. I didn't see any fireworks, bright lights, or hear a stadium of people cheering, but I definitely felt a new warm and loving Spirit was present in that cell. A loving Spirit the cold strong walls and bars could not keep out. I rolled over, hung my head over the side of the bunk and whispered, "You awake, Ty?"

"Of course, I'm awake. How can I sleep with all these angels hallelujahing around here? God bless you, Hunter Lowe. Welcome home."

Before I finally fell asleep I heard Tyrone say something under his breath. "Man, it's amazing how the Lord has to punch, push and twist the clay to remold some guys."

The next evening I was going to make a collect call to the folks, but in the mail that day I received a letter from Dad saying that Mom and he had accepted the Lord at Gwen's church three days ago. He also mentioned he didn't know why he still called it Gwen's church. "It's ours now," he wrote.

Walt Elwell, the adult Sunday school teacher, led them both to the Lord after a lesson in the class last Sunday. On top of my experience the night before, I knew now that when God works in our affairs, He does it in a big way. He really does care.

After breakfast, Tyrone and I sat at our little privately sanctified table in the chow hall. I felt a lot of questions coming out of me.

"Okay," I said, with my hands sliding flat on the table, "now that I've accepted Christ and want to be real about it, where do I start? I'm in the minority around here, ya know."

"Yeah, I hear ya. I know something about minority. Let's go back to the commons where we can talk."

When we got there, it was like going back to Tyrone's

classroom. "Here we go. Listen up now. Number one, read God's Word every day or as often as you can. The Bible is the only source of truth for a Christian. Don't make a big thing about it. Just read it and get to know God's plan for your life."

"All this *is* part of His plan isn't it?" I could see in a strange way the accident was part of the plan, even the beating, finding Tyrone, knowing Ben Marshall, hearing Gabe Jackson. God had given me time and space to do all my thinking. And knowing that the Lord was working in the lives of my folks at the same time, added to the blessing.

"I can see parts of the plan or puzzle," I said. "But why the death of Jill Marshall? That part, I sure don't get. Because of my selfish arrogance, God had to get my attention – and this is how He did it, didn't He? Wow, I and many others would have been better off if I'd listened to Gwen years ago. Right?"

Tyrone just listened as I figured it all out. Then he said, "God will heal the Marshalls in His time. We never will figure out the mind of God. Accept it, Hunt, and trust in Him." In somewhat of a sudden somber mood, Tyrone went on, "You're not telling me anything I don't already know, believe me. I know where you're coming from by thinking how you should have listened to others years ago, but let's go on.

"Number two on my list is your behavior. Other people in here or on the outside will know you're a Christian, and they'll read you like a book. They'll watch everything you do, and listen to everything you say. You represent Christ now, and you'll have to show it. You might be the only witness of Christ some people will ever see. What you say and do —that's what Christ is to them. It's a high calling, especially in here, but you can be proud of it."

I shook my head. "That sounds hard, but at the same time exciting. You feel that way around here?"

"It's hard, but it's the job God has given me now for the rest of my life. It gives me something worthwhile to do here. I hope I can keep it up."

"I'll be praying for you, Ty — the rest of *my* life."

"I'll be counting on that, Hunt. We're not done yet. Without knowing it, your behavior since your beating that first night has had an effect on Charlie. He still stomps around like the gorilla he thinks he is, but there's a dent in his animalistic personality. Hear how he refused to 'orientate' Seymour a few months ago? Said he's done beating up new guys. You put it there, even though he doesn't know it yet. You don't seem to hate him like his other victims, and you've never shown a desire to pay him back in any way. That calm, cool manner will serve you well in your witness.

"Number three comes when you get out of here. Become an active part in a church that teaches Jesus. It doesn't matter what the name over the door says. Do they teach Jesus? That's what you have to find out."

I nodded to show that I understood exactly what he meant. "And number four?" I asked.

"Number four is telling others about your faith. Not everyone will be glad to hear how you feel about Christ, but they'll be watching. Remember what Gabe Jackson said about being willing to speak up for Christ? Notice how confident he was? That brings us back to your behavior, or the way you act. You know, walk the talk."

I had not heard Tyrone talk in such detail about anything. He was deeply committed to getting me on the right track as a new believer. It was almost as if he wanted to see that I was going to carry out a job for him.

He kept going. "Before I got in here I was the baddest dude in the hood. They had to get me off the streets for the sake of the city. The only thing I knew about Jesus was that He was a good name to call on when I hated someone or something. Cursing came easy and meant something when I used His name. Yes, I regret all that now. But at the time, I was so full of hate and anger I didn't care who or what got in my way. I was such a spiteful worm. I was more afraid of living than dying. Most of my life had been spent playing in Satan's sandbox. I finally learned after too many years of hating myself and all the world that Satan cheats on everything. No one wins but him. He's selfish, doesn't share, and just takes all your good toys away.

"You notice how that visiting Preacher Crowley likes to talk to everybody? Even though I was as mean as I was, he always took time to talk to me. After a long friendship with the preacher, friendly on his part, he finally talked some sense into this bonehead I lived in, and I accepted Christ. Everything in my life changed. The whole world took on a new clean look. Even in this place.

"The most important change was that I lost all my

hate and fear of living. I'm looking forward to dying now, however long it takes the Lord to bring that to me. I feel I'm here to help guys like you to know the Lord, make your life worthwhile, and send you out of here. I'd like to help Charlie, but you've had a part of helping him, not me. Maybe our new buddy, Seymour, will come around.

"There isn't a guy in here from the warden to the dumbest inmate that hasn't noticed a change in my life. Everybody watches me, and they watch every minute. I'm sure they're just waiting for me to fall back into Satan's world. You think they looked at you before? Well, get ready, Hunt. They'll be looking at you again. You carry the reputation of Christ on your head."

Putting his hand on my shoulders, I could see Tyrone wanted to hug me, but knowing we were sitting in the middle of the commons he stopped short, and just said, "Wear your witness like a badge of honor. Wear it wherever you go. And, Hunt, wear it for me when you get out of here."

"Ty, how come you won't ever get out? What did you do that was so bad?"

"My dear young friend, let that question rest, rot, and rust right where it belongs — unknown. I'm sure somewhere in old man Pitts' files upstairs there's a big fat folder with the reason, many reasons. Honestly, I'm fully aware I deserve all this, but with Christ in my heart I only look ahead." Smiling and with a wink, he said, "My day of victory is coming. My body will rest in a pine box off in a corner of the prison yard, but I'll be free at last."

Chapter Twenty-Nine

Seymour really spiced up our little village in that concrete zoo. In a curious way we found him kind of fascinating and a new dimension in our existence. His language showed little improvement, and there was a decrease in the utter vile conjunctional phrases between the words. Just being in the vicinity of Tyrone Williams, Seymour seemed to lose his sharp edge and command of Satan's dictionary. Tyrone said I had a part in that, but I'm sure it was all Tyrone's doing.

At our table one day after Seymour had been here for about four months, he must have had a silent meltdown. He was actually a normal person to talk to. We asked if he were married or had any kids.

"Married?" he asked with a grunt. "Look at me. Ask that question again. Women have never had any interest in me that I can ever think of. They sure didn't line up on my porch to see me like they must have for Hunter here. As for kids? What do you think *that* answer is? Living in this short, fat, stubby carcass has been just one miserable day after another for as long as I can remember. Every day I got up and had to face that problem. The only thing that got people to pay attention to me was my mouth.

Just like all you guys. When I perfected the language arts, I went places — one crime after another and one jailhouse after another. My mouth just kept me digging a deeper hole."

Tyrone, in his usual intrusive way, said slowly, "I don't know why I'm black, but I've discovered no matter what or how I look, I know the Lord has a use for me. He made me this way. It's His job to use me as He wants to."

Seymour cocked his head and just looked at him. We wondered if another pile of nasty verbs, nouns, and adjectives were about to be spilled on the table, but some wise spirit blocked the flow. Instead we heard, "Now, take this here Hunter kid. He even looks good after the beating I heard he took a few years ago. He's tall and so well built that prison jump suit fits like it was tailored for him. I've noticed how other guys look at him. Even his face has healed up with that bad eye looking just like a permanent wink." Then he asked me directly, "Lowe, what was it like to grow up and live behind a handsome face and beautiful body like you had? You still have it you know. We uglies always wonder about that."

I nodded. "A few years ago I'd say it was great. People notice you, talk to you, want to be around you, and it's worth money — lots of money."

"Something I'd never know about," Seymour said.

Tyrone jumped in with, "Don't let those words impress you. Those good looks, great body, good money are just on the surface. It can all be taken away with one night in here — note the specimen in front of you."

"How do you see the world now?" Seymour asked me.

"From this place and at this table, I see the world like all the rest of you, concrete, bars, and noise."

Seymour went on with, "That's all I've ever seen for the past twelve years. You guys don't want to know what high school was like for me."

Tweedledum and Tweedledee jumped in quickly. "Yeah, yeah, I bet it was great," they said almost in unison.

"Awa, forget it. Ain't much. I shudda not said that."

"Can't stop now, Seymour," Tyrone said. "Tell us."

"Auntie Elaine told me when I was a baby I was cute, but by the time I got out of Junior high school and into high school all the cute was beat out of me. High school was just one bummer after another. I was always looked down at, really. I mean looked down on and made fun of by everybody. By kids and teachers. I dint have no close friends. Everybody avoided me, but they talked a lot about me. No dates, no clubs, no sports. Well, when they let me play baseball in gym class, they let me play second base — not the position, the base."

We all just laughed. Tweedledee said, "A guy can't be a base."

"I ain't kiddn' ya. They made me stand where second base should be and if the runner touched me they was safe. Trouble was, they dint just touch me, they hit me hard when they ran by or slid right into me. I looked like a wobbling bowling pin as I fell over. The coaches just laughed. When the yearbook guy had our picture taken, the coach said, "Eight, just write down the names of the guys, I don't want you in the picture." Any of ya want to ask why I quit high school?"

Now we were all laughing. Someone in the crowd gurgled out, "He was the second base."

I guess he was used to that reaction. Seymour went on with, "Hey, I told ya I come in from a different planet. One last thing, if ya gotta know all this. After I quit with the school, I got a night job cleaning the offices and warehouse of a greasy pre-owned auto parts dealership. That's a junk yard to you guys. Just me and Brutus. Now *he* was ugly. An ugly pit bull, but about the only real friend I had. After three months some stuff started to disappear. Want to guess who got blamed? Not Brutus. I was the one to lose the job. To this day, I don't where the stuff went.

"Well that's the time I turned to what I could do best, get into trouble anyway I could come up with. If I'm gonna be accused of stealing, I might as well do it. That got the career started that got me this home."

I was hoping Tyrone would step here in with some words of his wisdom – and he did. "Seymour, I sure don't know how or why God does what He does, but I know with everything in me, that God is not done with you. He has given you a gift that you don't know about yet, but He will bring it out someday."

In a quiet, shameful answer, Seymour lowered his head and said, 'Gift? I ain't ever got a gift – from God or nobody."

Gwen wrote to say that when she was home recently, she'd met Mr. John Hall who was now the principal of

Ravenswood High School. He told her that a week before he was in Capital City as a visiting Kiwanis club member. He was signing in when he met his old friend Dale Anderson, the former president of the modeling and entertainment firm, *Future Enterprises*, where I'd once worked.

Upon meeting, it seems their conversation included small talk about the trip to Capital City, and of course the weather. When seated at a table during the meal, they shared memories of their twenty-five to thirty years of friendship, family, job changes, and friends.

Dale Anderson brought up the memory of the meeting in Ravenswood seven years ago, and they laughed about my performance as Squeak, the village idiot, in the spring play. Apparently Dale Anderson told Mr. Hall that he laughed about my "Squeak speech" for days before offering me the job to become one of his models. Then, as the business grew bigger and the turnover for models was so fast he'd lost track of me.

"Dale, let's skip this business meeting," Mr. Hall had said. "Grab a cup of coffee and join me outside on the patio. I've got something to tell you I don't think you'll like to hear."

They took their cups out of the restaurant and for the next hour John Hall told his friend, Dale, the whole story about me from the accident: jail time, about the beating and my permanent disfigurement, right up to the point where he heard I'd had some type of religious experience. Mr. Hall told Gwen that he'd explained to Mr. Anderson that I was up for early release soon.

It seems that Dale Anderson could hardly believe what he was hearing, especially my new looks. He shook his head in a slow I-don't-want-to-believe-it motion, rubbed his chin, and explained that he used to be in the business of finding good-looking people for jobs. He reckoned that when he employed me he'd never seen anyone so well chiseled.

Dale suddenly stood up, flashed a look into John's face that made him blink, and explained how he'd wanted to get into a new business and he had another idea for "that young man." He'd sold his part of *Future Enterprises* and started a new business along the same line, but it only dealt with voices, not looks. He was calling it *Voice-Over, Inc.* It involved putting voices to a variety of CD and DVD uses.

He told Mr. Hall he would get in touch with some of his friends on the State Parole Board there in Capital City, and see what he could do for that kid again. I guess there was something about me he liked.

Chapter Thirty

After five years in this "joint," while working in the kitchen one day, Mike Gubbles, a guard right out of the warden's office staff, walked in and said a few words to the supervisor. Both of them then looked at me.

The supervisor yelled, "Lowe, you've got a date with Pitts. Now! Go with him."

"Why do I want to see Pitts? Something wrong?" I asked the guard.

"Not for you to ask the questions. You know the rules," Gubbles snapped. "And not for me to tell you why — even if I *did* know."

When we got into the warden's office, the warden told the guard, with a wave of his hand. "Gubbles, get a cup of coffee. Take a break."

"Sir, I can't leave you alone with an inmate. He's not restrained."

"Gubbles, get lost. I'll take the risk," the warden said harshly. "Lowe, take a seat. You'll want to be sitting down for this."

With a questionable frown and a tilted head, Gubbles left. The warden sat down, shuffled his short mature figure in his tall-back black leather chair. Clearing his throat he got straight to the point. "Hunter, the best part of this crummy hardheaded job I've got is that sometimes I get the pleasure of telling one of our inmates that his days here are shorter than he expected. Someone called Mr. Anderson has offered you a job, and he ..."

I felt I was hit in the face with another five gallons of ice water. Instantly my mind was outside the walls. *How soon will that be? Who is Mr. Anderson? I can see Gwen again. Mom and Dad will be glad. I can go back to Ravenswood. I can get a new car. I can buy things in stores and real clothes. These days are over. I'm outta here ...*

"Lowe! Lowe!" The warden's voice snapped me back to reality. "Do you hear me?" Pitts was almost in my face.

"Yes, sir, yes sir, I hear you. I'm sorry. I was just thinking about what — I'm sorry."

"Can't say I blame you. This has all come up fast. Somebody's pulling strings, or I should say, chains, because you're suddenly up for parole next time the board meets.

"Hunter, There are four reasons for your early release. First is your general good behavior. Second, the help you've been in the kitchen and other departments of this prison. Third, someone has offered you a job in Capital City. Fourth, we all think you're ready to leave here. You're not a threat to society. Personally, I never thought you should have been here in the first place. I have always been very proud of how you came out of that fight the first night. I regret not telling you this before.

Only a big man could have handled it like you did.

Usually we have to beg someone to give a man from here a job, and most of the time a guy has to go through a work release program. In your case, some businessman says he knows you, and he's willing to take full responsibility. I wish it worked like this more often."

"Who would want to give me a job looking like this?"

The warden, usually taken aback by a direct question from an inmate, calmly shuffled his frame and some paperwork. "In the first place, if I were you, I wouldn't question that. Secondly, a Mr. Dale Anderson, president of *Voice-Over, Inc.* has offered you a job and a handsome financial advance if you take some voice lessons."

Mr. Anderson? The name sounded familiar, but it didn't register right away. The news of possibly getting out soon blew my mind and left no room for rational thinking.

The warden closed the little meeting with, "You'll be hearing more details in about a week. Good luck, Lowe." With his right hand he shook my hand, and with his left pushed a button on his desk. "Gubbles, get back in here." Before he finished his call, the door flung open and Gubbles was at his desk.

When I started through the door, on the way out, the warden called after me, "Don't tell *anyone* for now, Lowe. These things have a way of blowing up in our faces."

Gubbles flashed a questioning look at the warden, shrugged at me, and said, "Let's go."

I felt like running and jumping all the way back to the

kitchen, but five years in here trained me how to walk through these halls with my head down. *How soon will this be? Who is Mr. Anderson?*

Chapter Thirty-One

Like the warden suggested, I didn't tell anyone, not even Tyrone. That was very difficult because we had shared our very souls to each other in the time I was there. But, not to jinx anything and have it all fall apart, I did just like Pitts asked. I kept my mouth shut, until one day at our table the news came from a surprising source.

Seymour, of all people, suddenly said out of the blue, "The walls been whispering around here that Lowe is gonna be getting out."

With a surprised and hurt look with a frown, Tyrone stiffened up, looked at me and said, "And you never told me?"

"Oh, Ty, I wanted to. I'm sorry, but Pitts told me not to tell *anyone*. You know how things like this fall apart. I was afraid to say or do anything to mess things up."

"I guess you're right. I know how it works. But I thought you'd have told me something like that first."

"Just no excuse, Ty. I'm sorry. By the way, Seymour, how did you of all people know what was going on? You're sort of new here."

Putting his hands behind his ears and spreading

them out more than usual, he said, "Look, with ears like these I pick up everything in these walls like radar. I even hear the mortar still curing."

It suddenly became known all over the cellblock. Some of the guys wouldn't talk to me. Many thought I hadn't served the time they thought I should have. They thought they should have gone before me. Together, Tweedledum and Tweedledee wished me good luck in the only way they could: they laughed and punched me around a little. Tyrone just smiled with a wishful face and Seymour just sat sad and silent with his big head in his hands.

After the guys in the cellblock all knew about my release, I made a collect call to the folks about the good news. They were as excited as I was. Dad told me he heard the news three days ago, but was also told not to let it be known. He also told me Mr. Anderson had contacted him to explain about the job offer. Dad said he took advantage of the opportunity on his own, and agreed to what Mr. Anderson wanted even without talking with me. When he knew the final date he said he would make arrangements with the Department of Corrections to pick me up and bring me back to Ravenswood or the Capital City, whichever I wanted. In the meantime I was not aware of all the maneuvering that had been going on between Dad, Mr. Anderson, the parole board, and the prison. Usually, I would have to be transported to Chicago for the release through that intake facility, but they all agreed to release me to my dad and Mr. Anderson right from here.

That same evening, several of us sat around our usual table after our turkey dinner and talked about the past five years. At lights-out time, Tyrone and I went to our cell and talked on through half the night. Tyrone clearly was happy for me, yet I couldn't help but feel he was hurting inside. The best-kept secret in that rumor mill was that none of us ever knew why Tyrone was in there without the chance of parole. Even the trained Wilts' ears never picked it up. Tyrone and I prayed a lot together that night, and again in the morning as we said our goodbyes. We both fought hard to hold back our emotions. We still couldn't show weakness, even at a time like that.

I packed up what little I owned into a black garbage bag and waited for John and his crew to come and get me for the walk to the processing unit. As I walked towards the door, a line of guys in prison jump suits waited to shake my hand, or slap me on the back with good wishes.

"Good luck, kid, you deserve it."

"You've done a good job here."

Seymour said, "Somewhere, somehow, I hope to see you again sometime."

Tweedledum said, "When you first came in here, I didn't think you'd ever make it out alive."

"Know it or not, kid, you've taught us all a few things."

"Go get 'em, Hunt."

"Don't forget us. Remember, you can visit sometime."

I could feel an affectionate grip in each hand — well most of them. That morsel of compassion was working overtime that morning, although I couldn't help noticing that the tough and hardened bunch of the crowd just stayed at their other tables. Some even looked the other way. When I got to the end of the hall, I suddenly remembered Charlie Sullivan. Charlie stayed in his cell, so I set my black garbage bag at a guard's feet and walked all the way back to him and stood in the doorway. He was facing the wall and in deep thought, running his fingers along the mortar joints around the cement blocks. I remember doing that same thing several years ago in Capital City, the day after the accident.

"Charlie," I said.

He turned towards me, tilted his head like a confused puppy, and for a minute we just looked at each other.

"Good luck, kid," was all he said, then nodded towards the exit as if I could go.

"I'll see you again sometime, Charlie."

"Dunno why ya should." He lowered his head and slowly turned back to the wall.

It was about noon by the time all the paperwork was done and I finally got changed into some real clothes. It was nothing like the top-of-the line clothes I modeled in, but a nice pair of kakis, a mock turtle neck sweater, and a dark blue blazer. I had forgotten what real clothes felt like. Then came the goodbyes to the guards. After five years in that place, there was a change in their attitudes. When I first came in there, it was, "Hey, you. Or hey, stupid, do this or that." Now, as we walked the through the gates and steel doors from unit to unit and building to building, without handcuffs, it was different.

"Good luck, Hunter. I've got the feeling we won't see you back here again," one of the guards at a desk said as I walked past him.

When Pitts shook my hand he said, "This is it, Hunter. I sure hope to see you again — but not in here."

Chaplain Derek added his final words with a whisper in my ear. "A word here from our old friend, Jeremiah. 'For I know the plans I have for you, plans to prosper you and not to harm you, plans to give you hope and a future.' God bless you, Hunter. Well done." Slapping his hand high on the door, he went on to say, "Beyond this door is your new life. I think you're going to enjoy your first view of it."

Chapter Thirty-Two

When the guard unbolted the door and swung it open, the weight of it caused the hinges to groan with a squeal in resistance. *I guess it doesn't like to let prisoners out.* When the door finished its swing, I squinted from a very bright sun high in the sky and felt a fresh, odor-free breeze on my face. I took a deep breath and filled my lungs with it. When I opened my eyes I saw a red mini bus and a group of people standing outside its open door. Boy, Dad sure made some arrangements.

First person I saw in front of the group was Gwen. Behind her were Mom, Dad, and Hannah whom I had not seen in five years. Also in the group were Aaron, Bruce, Reverend Crowley, and Reverend Johnson. Even Gwen's parents were there. Ben Marshall with his new wife and two kids held each other's hands tightly.

My chest heaved and my eyes got blurry as I ran to the crowd. With no handcuffs on it felt strange to be able to spread my arms wide like an eagle in flight — with a full garbage bag in one. With no shackles on my feet I could have flown the hundred feet to them. At last, I remembered what it was like to be free. Automatically, we all fell into a massive quivering group hug, with Gwen and me in the middle.

The slamming of the heavy steel door behind me made me shudder and shattered my bliss. When I whirled around at the familiar sound, and looked back I saw the same large dark old brick "dead end" wall and that ugly door I first saw five years ago. The wall was stark empty, the door closed, no one around. It was as if the world on the other side didn't exist. I felt I could have easily forgotten about all those I knew there. I was starting to enjoy my freedom, but the pain, loneliness, fears, and smells on the other side of those bricks continued — as it did every day without change, with or without me. A rebirth of life greeted me when I turned back to all those wonderful people standing around me.

Ben Marshall's kids were now young teenagers, and at last I had a chance to hold their hands and face them with my deep regrets. Marc was fourteen, and in a deep voice beyond his years said, "I really do wish you good luck. Dad told us that you've accepted Christ."

Kristin was thirteen, and she reached up and kissed me on the left cheek, the worst scarred part of my face. What an awesome moment of healing.

I turned to Ben. "Your kids are wonderful, Ben. You've done a good job."

"It's been a joy to know you, Hunter," Reverend Crowley said, as he came forward and embraced me. "I'm glad I had a part in your life. I can't go to Capital City with you, but I sure wanted to enjoy this moment together, and meet your family. I've never seen a welcome party like this. Hunter, in Jesus' name, the very best."

"Thanks, Pastor Crowley. You mean a lot to me. Hey, thanks for bringing Gabe Jackson here on that particular Sunday. Your timing was perfect. It made all the difference in my life that day to meet him and hear him sing those songs about Jesus."

"Hunter, it wasn't *my* timing that was perfect."

The bus was full of balloons, junk food, sandwiches (none made of turkey), and sodas, so we had a party on the way back to Capital City. I don't think a bunch of people could talk so much at the same time and still be heard. The new and happy atmosphere almost sent me into shock.

About an hour into the ride, as we were going by a small town park full of trees and small hills. I asked the driver to stop and told everyone on the bus, "I'm going to run up that hill over there. Any of you want to come with me?"

Hannah, Gwen, Aaron, and Bruce were out the door before I was. The others came out and just watched — even Ken the bus driver. We had only just met Ken, but he fit into this happy bunch of people like he belonged there. His grin and chuckle showed us he enjoyed the time as much as we did.

Holding hands, the five of us ran and jumped like seven-year-olds up the hill, around some trees and bushes, then through the tennis courts interrupting the players, putting them into a dignified huff. We didn't stop until we'd taken off our shoes and socks and had our feet dangling in a shallow pool of a fountain. Before anyone could speak, I took Gwen by the hands and asked her something I'd been rehearsing for five years. "Would you marry an ugly pirate like me?"

Without taking a breath I heard her answer, "I only see the Hunter Lowe I love. Yes, yes, Yesssss!" Her embrace bridged five miserable years and took my breath away.

Impetuous Bruce pushed Aaron into the pool. "Didn't I tell you he'd ask her that today?"

Wet up to his knees, Aaron was the first to congratulate us. Hannah ran back to the bus with the exciting news. "Hunter just proposed to Gwen. She said *Yes*. She said *Yes!*"

Now the party shifted into high gear, but it was no big surprise to anyone.

When we arrived in Capital City, Dad had reservations for us at Randy's Roundhouse, an old railroad roundhouse remodeled into a fine restaurant. One of the banquet rooms was decorated for our own private party. I insisted Ken, our driver, join us, and he said he'd be glad to. He'd only known this crazed bunch for a few hours, but he joined right in with the fun. He took off his red company tie, and bowing low held the door open for all of us as we left the bus. Mr. Anderson and his wife, Michelle, joined us at the restaurant, and we reintroduced ourselves to each other. His first words were, "Congratulations, Hunter. We'll talk Monday morning at my office. Let's eat."

Squeezing Mr. Anderson's hands, I said. "I don't

know how to thank you." I even surprised myself by not breaking down this time.

Right after a wonderful dinner without turkey — a real bad memory — I enjoyed real beef and ham. Aaron and Bruce had to get back to Ravenswood. Aaron, a dentist now, said to me, "I'd be glad to fix those broken teeth for you. It will all be on me, my gift to an old friend."

"Yeah, I have to get back home too," Bruce said. "My wife is in her final days of pregnancy. I took a chance on being away from her for the day as it is, but, hey, for you I'd do it."

I found it hard to imagine Aaron and Bruce in their new lives. To me, they were still the same crazy guys I had known years before. Gwen's folks, my folks, Gwen, and I spent a wonderful weekend in Capital City. On Sunday we attended Pastor Johnson's and the Marshall's church, where we met many great new friends. I met a bunch of people there who said they prayed for me for five years, ever since the accident that ruined Ben and Jill's marriage. I had the joy of thanking all of them face to face. I had a rough time facing those new and wonderful people while conscious of how I looked. I certainly learned fast how to grin in a pleasant way without showing a mouth some missing teeth. It was obvious they understood, by their true friendliness.

That Sunday afternoon I bought some more clothes with my new "support group." I let Gwen pick out a few shirts she wanted to see me in. Although I didn't need glasses, I bought a pair of shaded eye glasses that did a pretty good job of covering up the slightly closed eye and some scars on the side on my head.

On that Sunday evening everyone left to return to Ravenswood. I spent the first evening of my freedom alone in a small single room efficiency apartment Mr. Anderson and Dad had gotten for me. Five years ago, that first night, alone on the floor in the county jail of this city, had been the first of many dark nights of my life. This night, also alone, was one of the brightest. I didn't hear loud cussing voices, doors slamming, buzzers, or country and western music on cheap radios. The silence, the muffled traffic noises, clean sheets and a soft mattress kept me awake. To my surprise, I enjoyed looking at the drapes.

Chapter Thirty-Three

Monday morning I was at Mr. Anderson's office, where I was finally able to ask him, "Just how did you find me and decide you wanted me to work for you?" He told me about the day he ran into Mr. Hall at the Capital City Kiwanis meeting and the conversation they had with the memories of the meeting when I was at Ravenswood where I spoke.

"I remember that day for another reason, Hunter. Not only were you so good looking, but your regular voice, as you talked about the school, had a deep resonating tone and quality, very natural and pleasant to listen too. In this business it's the type of voice we look for. From your Midwestern origins, you don't have an accent we have to get out of you."

"Can your people work with an ex-con?"

"I've told them all about the accident and your past. I also told them if I ever hear or see a problem with that, they will have to answer to me — directly. They *will* work with you."

"I'm not sure I'll be able to speak the way you want me to before I get my new teeth."

"We'll do the training, and work them in as you get them."

The opportunity of working with real people without hearing, "Hey you, Stupid" at every turn was a pleasure. The feel of soft carpet under my feet was a buzz, and the claustrophobic acoustics of the recording rooms almost burst my ears. The echoes of loud talking, slamming iron doors, and the ugly mixture of noises I was used to hearing were gone. In a few weeks I was able to get a driver's license and a good used car, with some help from a car dealer in the church. Getting a good used car was one thing, the insurance another. Not too many companies want to work with an ex-con driving. I learned Mr. Anderson stepped into that issue, also with a friend. I was always surprised by what others did for me.

Not wanting to face too many friends back in Ravenswood yet, I snuck into town a few times to see Gwen and the family. The old neighbors were glad to see me, and we talked a lot about "the good old days."

In these visits Aaron worked over my tooth problem and I had a chance to meet Bruce's wife and baby son. What a pure and precious joy to hold a sleeping, warm, wrapped up sixteen pound bundle of innocence after so many years of being among tough guy stuff in a prison.

Tyrone kept up a letter writing promise to me, better than I to him, and he told me that of all people, Seymour Wilts was opening up to his witness. They were having serious conversations about Christ, and Seymour was about to follow me in becoming a "jailhouse Christian."

171

Tyrone told me there was nothing bad or wrong with that title. After all, both of us bear that label too. It's just that a jail is about the hardest place to witness and live for Christ. There is so much against a person for being a Christian. Most people think it's all a game just to get favors or less time. Those same people use a lot Jesus words they've heard from others, to try and sound good.

No matter what some people think, becoming a Christian is not an easy way out of jail. Prisoners who have a genuine conversion and love of Jesus feel obliged to confess to crimes for which they have not been convicted. This can result in a longer sentence.

Tyrone wrote, "Seymour picked up that same attitude that Gabe Jackson did: 'I don't care who knows I'm a Christian.' He sure isn't as big as Gabe, as you know, but his mouth has been converted to very quick remarks about his faith. His mouth is tame now, but there is still a little leftover Wilts' vocabulary. Sometimes I think I've witnessed Saul becoming Paul."

Gwen and I planned our wedding on these little visits, and we decided to call Capital City our home. My job was there, and Gwen could get a job at one of the big hospitals. I knew Gwen always wanted a big church wedding with all the bells and whistles, but there were a lot of reasons to keep it simple. She was really happy to just have an old fashioned wedding with a small reception in the fellowship hall of the church.

I told her, "Paying thousands for lots of people to pig-out on cold roast beef and string beans, and then forget the dinner, is not my idea of being smart. It doesn't make anyone more married."

She said many times that it would be just for family and few close friends. The wedding would be in Ravenswood, of course at Gwen's church. Her best friend, Becky, now Becky Zimmerman, would be matron of honor, and my sister Hannah a bridesmaid. Aaron and Bruce would be co-best men. The whole thing was a little unusual, but it worked.

On our way down to the lower level of the church for a simple reception, Bruce told Gwen and me to look outside. So much for a simple, quiet wedding. Standing in the parking lot were about fifty old friends from around the town and high school. They all came in and enjoyed a large buffet set up to accommodate them also. The tables were all set up, and additional cake was available. The work of Aaron and Bruce, I'm sure.

Besides a lively reception, it was a happy and spiritually rich wedding. Because of my sensitivity and the embarrassment of my looks, pictures were kept to a minimum, but Bruce's one-year-old son kept the event tuned to the max. It added a special new-life touch to the day.

The increasing work loads of our jobs kept us from having an exotic honeymoon, so we honeymooned in Peoria. It wasn't Hawaii or Paris, but it was ours. When we were there, we learned that Peoria is known to be the oldest community in Illinois. After what seemed to be years of hope smashed in tragedy, and years of difficult waiting, Peoria looked good to us.

Mr. Anderson personally helped me a great deal in

the voice-over work. He got the accounts, and negotiated contracts. He also got the scripts and had the speaking and editing done in his studios. I didn't have to meet the clients, and it worked out well for all concerned. The customers were satisfied.

My voice narrated many vacation DVDs for travel agencies, and it was my voice on dozens of training DVDs and CDs for local manufacturers and corporations. I had to consult special dictionaries and learn to use difficult words when asked to do voice-overs for law firms and medical centers. I came to realize the truth about good hard work and the comfort of doing something worthwhile. And that was a great feeling. One day, Mr. Anderson came to me with an idea that would shift my incredible life into yet another orbit.

Chapter Thirty-Four

The executives of a nationwide insurance company named *Your State Insurance* were thinking about a new series of ads featuring an impish squirrel that would try and cause accidents by his mid-road indecisions. Then he'd be upset and angry when he found out the owner of the car had *Your State Insurance*. They needed a different and unique voice for "Skeeter," the squirrel. Mr. Anderson remembered that day, several years ago when I spoke at the Kiwanis Club in Ravenswood about my part in the school play. I was the village idiot, Squeak, and spoke in a broken, high pitched voice with a Cajun accent. Mr. Anderson wanted to enter a few of us from his company into the auditions and tryouts for the nationally known insurance company. Voices could only be entered on CDs.

Hundreds of well-known personalities and unknowns were in the running, and after three months of sifting through all the entries, my voice doing Squeak was chosen. Months later, after the competition, I learned that it was a unanimous choice from the panel gathered in Phoenix. The public relations people at the insurance company wanted a big promotion on this, but Mr. Anderson, in his manipulative and creative way got them to keep the personality of the voice a secret. Those same public relations people never even saw me. It all added to the mystique of Skeeter.

"Besides," he said, "this whole squirrelly idea probably won't even get up the tree. Let's not make a big deal about it."

However, the insurance company executives bought into the idea, and the pilot ads were started in several different states. To the surprise of everyone, the commercials went viral and exploded in our faces. The ads went over like the Fourth of July.

Within weeks it was a success. In months I was only doing Skeeter ads for all different sections of the country, to meet the needs of *Your State Insurance Company* in various locations. We had fun with all this, and it brought good income for us, more customers for *Your State*, and their stock went through the roof. The company knew a bonanza, and Skeeter moved into home and life insurance ads. I was Skeetering my voice all day, and some overtime to keep up with the demand. I was the only one who could do it to their standards.

Further promotions, which led to more money for the insurance company, were Skeeter Candy, Skeeter Nuts, Skeeter Tails for car antennas and caps. Skeeter Lunch Boxes for kids, Halloween costumes, bumper stickers, window stickers, and Skeeter clothing like T-shirts, jackets, and even underwear. But I couldn't model for them. Clothing manufacturers made shorts for kids with bushy squirrel tails on them. There were Skeeter mugs with bushy tails for handles, and Skeeter was a big hit in parades. Schools and clubs held contests to see who could sound most like Skeeter. Yearbook themes were built on Skeeter. The whole deal became a national frenzy.

"Hunter, I think we've gone over the edge on this," Mr. Anderson told me one day. "It's time to get back to the real world. Keeping all this a secret is hard on all of us."

"You don't know how glad I am to hear you say that," were my first words in response. "How are we going to stop it?"

Thousands and thousands of people around the country began to make it an issue for the insurance company to acknowledge who the famous voice belonged to. They didn't really like the pressure to name the voice, yet the publicity was a free offshoot of the ads. Guesses included actors, comedians, and politicians. When the insurance company announced that the voice was an "unknown," the guessing stopped, but the intensity now had everybody wondering about their own neighbors, relatives, or friends. Mr. Anderson and the insurance company executives knew this had to come to a close, so word was sent out that on August first, the voice of Skeeter would be revealed by a public news conference from Chicago. I was ready for the pictures by now.

Five months after our honeymoon in Peoria and in our apartment in Capital City, one evening we were curled up on the couch watching some lame game show on TV. Gwen slid closer to me, rubbed her hand through my hair, but said nothing. It was a touch that broadcasted, "I've got something to tell you."

"What's all this about," I said.

She took off my glasses and bore her eyes right into mine. "How'd you like to be a father?"

I just looked at her.

"Answer me. You want to be a daddy?"

Embracing her. "Of course. Of course. When is the little one due?"

"Not a little one. *Two* little ones!"

"How'd that happen so fast?"

"Hunter, lover, you know how that happened. He, she, they are due in late August sometime."

Suddenly we didn't care who won the game on TV.

The tenth reunion or our high school class was to be held in Ravenswood at our old high school in the new cafeteria on July thirtieth. I was asked to be there and share my story with all my old friends. I was looking forward to this opportunity of telling them that regardless how I looked now, the real change in my life was on the inside. Mr. Anderson also said I could sneak the announcement about Skeeter to them — if they would be quiet. Yeah, right.

Tyrone's letters came at a regular clip, bless his heart. I answered about one to his every three. He said he understood I must have really been busy with everything in my life, and he had the time. His letters usually were full of information about what was going on in the cellblock even thou the daily life was always just the same old stuff.

His most recent letter was the most bizarre. Seymour was suddenly transferred out, really out. He wrote, "I don't know how the state bureaucracy works at all. Seymour was never supposed to be here at Putnam Prison in the first place. His sentence for armed robbery and assault was really up, but some administrative officer in Chicago didn't like his mouth and shuffled the papers so he would end up here for who knows how long."

Tyrone wrote, "Seymour, being the guy he was, didn't know the difference and never said or expected anything else. In the weeks before his release he accepted the Lord and began to read the Bible and other books of mine all the time. Boy, did the others get on his case. Like I said in the last letter to you, he took on the attitude of Gabe Jackson and just didn't care what others thought of him. I guess he had a lifetime of learning that skill. He used the talent and force of his natural voice to do his witnessing. As he read the stories in God's word, he found them not only fascinating stories of faith, but from his dizzy background, he also found funny things about them."

He went on to write, "Chaplain Derek got him into a halfway house in Colorado Springs, Colorado, called *Lost Reclaimed*. There he got the support and encouragement he needed. Get this   he has learned that his mouth truly was his gift. He is learning how to become a Christian comedian — it fits. That mouth we heard so much vile language from has been converted also. You'll hear him sometime. He definitely has a way of bringing God's Word to people through humor. He has claimed Acts 2:28 his verse: *You have made known to me the paths to life; you will fill me with joy in your presence.* What a shame he was sent here at all."

At that point I set the letter down, grabbed a tablet and wrote a quick note to him saying, "Tyrone, you of all people should know this is how God works. Seymour and I were sent to Putman so we could meet you, and you could bring us to the Lord. Your ministry goes on and on, lived out in those who hear Seymour or me. You can't go to others, so the Lord brings the likes of us to you. There are others in there just waiting for the moment. Keep up the good work. Keep fishing."

Chapter Thirty-Five

A year after I was released, and one month before my tenth year high school reunion, I received an email from Reverend Crowley asking if I'd return with him to the prison some Sunday afternoon to be a part of his services and give my testimony. I felt honored to be asked, yet disturbed at the same time with the thought of returning to that place where one of my lives ended. After thinking it over, and remembering how many people had helped me and forgiven me, I knew it was my duty and privilege to help the fisherman do some fishing. Besides, I would see Tyrone again.

It was raining monsoon style as I drove into the prison parking lot that Sunday, and I had to run with a newspaper over my head to the outer gatehouse where I met the preacher talking to the guards. He introduced me to them, and one said, "I remember you. You're the one that got into that awful fight your first night here. That must have five or six years ago. How's it going?"

"Six to be exact, but who's counting," I said with a grin.

"You really got a bad rap for a first offender."

"Especially that fight," the other guard put in. "We remember that one. Some of us still talk about it. It really messed you up, didn't it? You know Charlie Sullivan is still here. You plan to see him?"

"Yeah, that fight taught me some things the hard way. I suppose I'll see him. I don't know how things will go. Okay, I hope."

I thanked them for their interest and concern. I had the feeling at last the guards and I were on the same side.

Reverend Crowley and I jogged through the rain that had let up, to the next set of gates where we met other guards, answered more questions and signed in. I knew I'd be walking out in a few hours, but bad memories jumped back at me as we passed through one familiar set of doors after another. The familiar buzzer sounds returned to me.

We finally reached the office of Chaplain Derek, and he thanked us for coming. He was always thankful for Reverend Crowley's visits, because the preacher would speak straight and frank about the gospel – and never hold back when telling the men of the hope in Jesus.

The chaplain had to choose his words carefully because of state mandates, and always had to be politically correct. I found it strange that in a prison where the inmates have broken every rule in the book, and couldn't care less what people say, the chaplain can't "offend" anyone with what he says. Reverend Crowley, the fisherman, was always fishing and although he didn't bring 'em in like Peter, he'd have success with one "fish" at a time – like Tyrone – and then he kept fishing.

A few more doors opened and slammed shut behind us, and we were finally in the little theater, among a crowd of about fifty guys. I saw a few new, scared faces and I wondered what kind of a story was behind each of them. The men that I did know just said a word or two of greeting. I met Tweedledee and he told me Tweedledum was released. He looked like a guy without his right arm.

For the most part it wasn't a festive occasion — prison never is. I was glad to see Tyrone there with his big smile and unashamed bear hug. I never understood, but always admired his Christian attitude, even though he'd never know another breath of fresh air in his lungs. As close as we were when I was there, I never learned Tyrone's whole story. I hurt deeply for the guy and loved him like a brother.

Because of the noise level it was obvious most of the inmates were in the theater because of nothing else to do. It was a chance to get out of their cells and walk around. I could see there were only about eight who came to sincerely worship with their Bibles, and it was because of them Reverend Crowley made his usual Sunday afternoon visits.

I guess the preacher would rather have been home with his family, but he knew how much these few men depended on him. He would often bring a visitor or two, like the day he brought Gabe Jackson I remember so well. Sometimes he'd bring a singing group or someone who could really play the piano. Once in a while he would bring a married couple, but he was never comfortable with having a woman in there. He didn't know how the men would react.

As I entered, I saw Charlie Sullivan on his usual perch in the windowsill. I wondered how soon he'd be leaving the theater today. As I walked by him, I tried not to look his way, but since I had found Jesus and knew what He could do to Charlie and how He forgave others, I looked at him and nodded.

I heard his low, strong voice. "Hi, kid." And he stuck out his hand. While twisting around to shake it I almost tripped over my own feet.

"Hi, Charlie," stumbled out of my mouth. *That's enough for now.* A few steps later I sat at one of the front seats, and said to Tweedledee, "What's with Charlie? He almost seemed civil."

"He's getting soft in his old age. He remembers he gave up beating new comers after he did you in."

Just before Reverend Crowley got up to the simple podium that only held a cheap state-issued plastic pitcher of ice water, he whispered to me, "Today I'm going to speak about the victory in Jesus we can all know, regardless of our condition. Would you find a way to use the word 'victory' in your testimony — just to tie things together?"

"Sure."

To start with he introduced himself, and told the crowd how long he'd been doing this, and how much he enjoyed it because he felt it was part of his ministry. We sang a couple of songs from the old wrinkled handouts.

"Play it again, Sam," aka our Jewish piano player, attempted to flaunt his skill at that old upright piano pulled from a storeroom. It was Sammy's time to shine and stand out in the only way he knew how. If music is supposed to enhance worship, Sammy had a tough time making that piano cooperate.

Sure enough, Reverend Crowley spoke about victory. The victory that the apostle Paul knew over the rough treatment he experienced in the places he preached at, and the times he spent in various prisons. The preacher told them that any of them could know victory, even here. He spoke his usual seven minutes to fit into their attention span. Then without skipping a beat he laid it on me with, "Most of you remember Hunter Lowe who lived here for a while, until a year ago. I've asked him to come back and share his testimony and any other thoughts he might have."

Chapter Thirty-Six

When I stepped up to the front, four or five guys clapped their hands and whistled in a mediocre attempt to be funny. I thanked the preacher and all of them for this opportunity, and assured them I wouldn't take long. I did have to admit that the promise resulted in a few cheers.

"Like the preacher said, I did live here for a while. I got to know Tyrone, Tweedledee, Charlie Sullivan, and a lot other guys. Some of you are here this afternoon. Foolishly I got drunk one night, and while driving home at two in the morning I broadsided another car and killed the mother of two kids. I spent five years here for that carless moment and I deserved every one of them."

Because I believe a testimony should come from the heart, and be short, I didn't have any notes to look at. It was just their faces in mine. I started by quoting 1 Corinthians 15:57. "But thanks be to God! He gives us the victory through our Lord Jesus Christ." I continued with, "The apostle Paul was talking about the victory of our new life in Christ. Some of us are living new and victorious lives because we know that God cares for us. The word victory itself means to win the prize, but for some of us here all we've known is losing. The victory in Jesus that we speak of is victory over the battles in our lives. Sometimes those battles land us in a place like this, and sometimes those battles go on only deep in our hearts and minds. Sometimes we fake it so well that others don't even know the battles we fight.

"They could be battles over guilt, anger, depression, loneliness, failure, physical addictions, the feeling of being deserted, or a hundred others." *Well, I've started. Most of these men are older than me. I wonder how they're taking this. I see some of them looking at me as if they want to believe it, but haven't heard enough yet.* The sound of buzzers, doors closing and distant voices constantly echoing in the distance, reminded me that the routine of prison life still goes on, Sunday or not.

"When I was a kid and a teenager I had it pretty good on the outside, but there was always a feeling I was fighting something deep inside. I discovered it was the battle for my soul. Satan, yes he's real, would have us believe we don't need Jesus or His forgiveness in our lives. For most of my life I thought I had it all. I had looks good enough to get paid for it, cars, money, friends, and all that stuff. I was fully satisfied and I didn't need Jesus. I found out one night in a car wreck that can all be taken away with screeching tires and a heavy thud of a human body against metal.

"God made us with an enormous desire for inner peace. Inside your hearts many of you fight this same battle. I know, I stood in your shoes for several years here having to act tough, but still wanting peace. Many of you are tough and rugged on the outside. You have to be. You're living a phony life, but screaming for peace in your heart. That peace," I said pointing at them, "is in the victory we can have in Jesus. A few guys here know it."

I glanced at Charlie Sullivan and noticed he'd not moved a muscle in the last ten minutes. *Did he die?* I kept on speaking. "Regardless of how good or bad a person is, we all must answer the knocking of Jesus at the door of our heart. Without Christ, men serve only Satan, and either end up dead, living a useless life, or like I said, in a place like this. You've all avoided death so far, so consider that to be evidence that Jesus still cares about you, and can give you victory over a sinful and messy life. Wasn't it baseball catcher Yogi Berra who said, 'It ain't over till it's over?' He was right. It's not over till it's over. And if you're still breathing here in front of me today, you still have the chance to know the peace and victory God wants you to have. Remember our little friend, Seymour Wilts?"

Many laughed and shook their heads.

"Amen," came from Tyrone.

I concluded with an invitation. "You can invite Jesus into your life at any time and know that victory. Make it now. The preacher, Tyrone, and I will help you."

Reverend Crowley asked Sammy to go to the piano and play *Victory in Jesus*. "The song is new to most of you and quite fast, so I'll ask Sammy to play it through once."

With Sammy's desperate attempts at the piano, the guys all stood up and struggled through the first verse. It was fast all right. It sounded like someone telling his story about coming to Jesus, a song like I remembered Gabe Jackson singing about two years ago when he got my attention. The song writer told of an old, old story about a Savior – Jesus – who came from glory and gave His life on a cross – to save a wretched creature like me. Jesus groaned and suffered a lot, and His wonderful blood saved me from my sins – and I ended up with the victory.

The singing was a gallant effort by the prisoners. They were certainly trying. When the chorus came up and the second verse began, the song seemed to fall into place and sounded better than the verse before.

The story went on about His healing and cleansing power that made a crippled guy walk and blind people to see. If Jesus could do that, I knew He could heal the broken spirits here – as He did for me, when He gave me the victory.

The next verse was better yet. I even think it gave some of the prisoners a wisp of hope. The song told about a mansion built for us in heaven where the streets are gold and the ocean is like crystal. Angels keep singing the redemption story, and someday I know I'll be singing the song of victory myself. The chorus of this song said that victory is in Jesus forever.

As the song progressed, Sammy seemed to do better with the melody. The preacher and I caught each other's eyes and at the same time felt the shiver of the Holy Spirit. The song and singing became a pleasant sound as it echoed back to us off the block walls.

When the singing finished, a loud voice from the back of the theater yelled, "Sing it again!" The voice was familiar, but I didn't question it. I looked at Sammy. "Chorus again, Sam."

Chapter Thirty-Seven

"*O Victory in Jesus ...*" With all the bluster of a tornado, that voice again filled the theater. *"Papa!"* It was Charlie Sullivan, calling to his earthly father. As he shuffled his way to the front, without being told what to do, all heads swiveled to watch him — even the guards. In his moment of conviction I felt his mind was set on his soul, not on controlling the prison.

The strange event played itself out in slow motion. Within seconds Charlie was standing directly in front of me, a broken man with a face full of tears running down that ugly beard. I stood there with the same feeling Ananias must have had when he heard Saul was coming to his house. Behind Charlie everyone was standing in rapt attention, the guards too.

Now in a much softer and pleading tone of voice, Charlie said to me, "Will Jesus take even me?"

Somewhere between joy and fright, I managed to say, "Yes, Charlie, even you."

"But why would Jesus want to save my sorry face?"

Leaning over to touch his sunken shoulder, I said, "Simply because He loves and cares for you, Charlie."

"Even after what I done to you and all them other guys?"

"Charlie, Jesus loves you. Always did, always will. He's not too excited with what you've done with your life, but He still loves you. How many times have you heard, 'He loves you so much, He died for you'?"

"Lot's times from Papa. But I don't know why He done that."

"The love thing, Charlie, the love thing. Now you're getting it. Remember the little song you used to sing, *Jesus Loves Me*? Well, there ya go. You knew He loved you when you were a boy in your Papa's little Pentecostal church. He still loves you today, right where you stand. The end of the matter and the answer to your question is yes, Jesus can save even you."

Charlie stood there with his head down and body trembling. "I don't get it. I just don't get it."

I put my hands on his quivering shoulders and went on. "Charlie, listen to the memories of your Papa. He spoke the truth whether you liked it or not. Your way sure didn't work, did it? Our God is the Lord of the second chance, the Lord of mighty forgiveness. Our God is the only God that offers grace to the sinner. He doesn't even demand a simple sacrifice from us. He did the sacrificing Himself for us. Nobody has to work or buy His grace and forgiveness. Just accept it through Jesus Christ."

My eyes were fixed on Charlie only. The theater could have been empty or full for all I knew at that moment. "Let me give it to you straight, Charlie. When Jesus said,

'It is finished.' He meant He defeated Satan in your life. If you, or anyone, don't accept Jesus' sacrifice on the cross, you're doomed to an eternal hell."

With his head tilted like a puppy, and eyes flushed clean of hatred by tears, Charlie whimpered, "You sure? He can save even me?"

"Everybody on earth must make the choice to accept God's forgiveness for themselves. No one can make the decision for them. No granny, grandpa, mom, or dad. No Sunday school teacher, aunt, uncle, or preacher can make you a Christian. Charlie, you and you alone, 'must be born again.'"

Quietly, Charlie asked me another question. "I heard all this before from my papa didn't I? Kid, I want what you got. Can you show me how to get Jesus in me?"

We went to some chairs and sat down in the front row right there in the theater and I said to him, "If you're serious, Charlie, repeat after me. Dear Lord Jesus,"

"Dear Lord Jesus,"

"I am a sinner and I need Your forgiveness."

"I a sinner and a real bad guy, and I gotta have forgiveness."

"I believe You died for my sins."

"I know You died for my sins."

"I want to turn from my sins."

"I want to turn from my sins and my nasty life." Charlie took a deep breath, but I could see he wanted to go on, so I continued.

"I now invite You to come into my heart and my life."

"Now I'm beggin' You to come into my crummy

heart."

"I want to trust You as Savior and follow You as Lord."

"I want to trust You as my Savior and Lord — like Papa wanted me to."

When we stood up I found myself wrapped up in the burley and smelly arms of Charlie. Not being beaten up this time, but as a brother. The whole atmosphere of the theater was surreal, quiet, and seemed to stand still. Everyone just looked on in silence, even the guards. I never thought tears could come from that man. Then he surprised us all, most of all me. With his fingers, he wiped his tears then tenderly took my face in his big rough, gorilla-type hands and softly touched every scar he put there six years ago. He also softly touched my half closed eye. If he had the gift of healing, I'd been restored. With each affectionate movement he spoke. "I'm sorry, I'm so sorry. You got forgiveness for Charlie?"

Could I ever forgive him for what he did to me? I didn't want to at first, but like the snapping of a finger, or the cuffing of my head, the Lord reminded me that He forgave me. The Lord also reminded me of how Ben Marshall forgave me for what I did to him and his family. "Yes, Charlie, I forgive you. I even love you now."

The quiet and reverence remained in the theater as some inmates shuffled off to the chow hall. Charlie, the preacher, Tyrone, and I were talking about another visit when Charlie suddenly interrupted in his crude and old demanding way.

"Baptize me!"

"What?"

"Baptize me! A new Christian gotta be baptized, don't he?"

The preacher took over at once. "Charlie Sullivan, upon your confession of faith, I now baptize you in the name of the Father, the Son, and the Holy Spirit."

He reached for the pitcher of water on the podium and poured it, ice and all, on Charlie's head. Those left in the crowd cheered, yelled, and whistled. As the echo of the excitement filled the entire prison, the guards stiffened up.

The sight of Charlie standing there with water and tears streaming down his face, though his ugly beard and broken teeth was a picture that no camera recorded, but would stay with many of us for life. The preacher held up his hand and called for quiet. "This is what it's all about, guys. Listen, 'I tell you that, in the same way, there is more rejoicing in heaven over one sinner who repents than over ninety-nine righteous persons who do not need to repent.' That's from Luke 15:7, and what we see going on here is also going on in heaven right now too."

Chapter Thirty-Eight

The inner workings of that medium security prison always baffled me. At times they were all "'by the book" with handcuffs, shackles, no visitors after an event. Yet once-in-a-while, open to surprises. Such was the case after that service in the theater that day. Somehow I think the low key way Warden Pitts ran the place worked its way down the chain of command; through chains, of course.

After that service where Charlie Sullivan proved that concrete walls and steel bars cannot keep God out, my old "friend" John was now the assistant warden, the one who ran the place when Pitts was not around. He actually invited the preacher and me to dinner, a turkey dinner of course. That morsel of compassion had swelled up again.

Tyrone, the preacher, Tweedledee, and I sat at one of the circular tables. John even let Charlie join us at the table for the first time in years. Other guards didn't think much of the idea, so they watched us like hawks. Several others stood around us in another break with the rules. To me this was all just a sample of how God's Spirit can work if left free to run His course.

As soon as the trays were set down, Tweedledee started in talking about Seymour. "You'd be proud of the little guy, Lowe. Tyrone has kept in touch with him and tells us he's doing real good at that place he's in. Ya know, he was here by mistake. Can you believe that?"

"Yes, I think I can," I said. "How's he doing?"

"Better let Tyrone tell ya. He talks better than all of us."

Looking at Tyrone, "Well?" I asked.

"Hunter, God healed that potty mouth like he made blind men see and crippled men walk. At *Lost Reclaimed,* Seymour got himself pulled together and grew in the faith thanks to the counselors and other ex-cons living there. He began to put his experiences of his awkward life into funny stories. He also applied funny stories to God's events in the Bible. Not in a sacrilegious way, but with messages guys in a place like this and kids in high schools could understand. Seymour discovered his creative mouth *was* his gift and he's now using it to witness through humor."

The pastor added, "He's still new at relating to 'normal people' and traveling around the country, but I invited him here a few months ago to try out his gig on these guys."

From one of the inmates standing behind us, "Hey, Ty, tell Hunter what the skunk thought just before the car hit him."

"Okay. What *did* he skunk say just before he was hit?"

"The way you're driving, you might turn me into a

pile of road kill, but when I die, I'll leave you something to talk about for a long time."

"Tell him about when God was done with making the animals He thought He could do better so He made a man and woman. Seymour was funny when he told how Adam named the animals as God lined them up in front of him. That one made me laugh for a week."

"Lowe," another one said, "his funniest story was what Adam thought when he first saw Eve, just the two of them alone in the woods with no clothes."

"Get this," another broke in. "The little guy started his story about the creation of beautiful animals like the horse, swan, soaring eagle, and that kind. Then he talked ugly: amarillo, opossum, lobster, moose, rats, bats, and himself. He said, 'When I'm introduced as Seymour Wilts, and I waddle out on the stage like Number Eight, I already have the people laughing.'"

The preacher couldn't help himself. "Now remember, guys, all that funny stuff also tells us that God has a sense of humor, but He uses it all to bring about His purposes." Turning to me, "Hunter, Seymour puts himself into that ugly bunch with love. He said, 'My face, ears, size, waddle and most of all my mouth, got me into this place and now they all work together to make you guys laugh. Enjoy a moment out of your bad days, and testify to the Lord.'"

Tyrone listed a few of Seymour's story lines, and as he mentioned each one, the guys at the tables standing behind us and from other nearby tables all laughed. Like the problem Noah had with the piling up mess in the bottom of the ark. He couldn't throw it overboard, 'cause he knew some day the E.P.A. would get on his case about polluting the lakes and streams. Noah also had a problem keeping the skunks happy and tried to stop the hyenas from laughing all the time. Noah never could find the snail, spiders, ants, and other bugs, but he figured they'd take care of themselves. Where the fly and mosquitoes were didn't bother him at all. The hole he had to make in the roof for the giraffes was a problem at first when it was still raining. He was glad it was only forty days. The elephants were getting restless.

Tyrone told the story of what Seymour told them about Paul and Silas in prison. Seymour even knew what song they were singing.

"What song was it?" I had to ask.

He broke into a well sung rendition of, "Every day with Jesus, is sweeter than the day before, every day…" Charlie, still not accustomed to enjoying conversations added, "Then a earthquake busted up the joint, but all the cons just stayed there. Yeah, right, like I'd stay here if this joint fell apart."

"You'd have to be there," some voices in the crowd said. "Seymour was really great. Ya couldn't help but love the little guy."

In about an hour of that extra pleasure the guards finally asked the pastor and me to leave. But not before I was able to say, "Listen to Tyrone here, and remember our little friend. He might be funny and make people laugh, but like all of us he probably holds on to some baggage of the past."

On my drive back to Capital City, although it might

be short notice, I thought I'd see if I could get Seymour to come with me to my tenth reunion of the high school class, and help liven up that bunch. They could use his type of humor.

Chapter Thirty-Nine

One advantage of living behind a badly marked face like mine is that I don't have to look at it. In prison it wasn't too bad. Most faces there were scarred or torn because of rough lifestyles. Tattoos and other "body art" marks were normal, but once on the outside people always seemed to make a double take when they saw me. Sometimes little kids in a mall or store would point to me. Older kids would laugh and make some snide remark in passing. I'd like to have told them the whole story, but I quickly found out that very few people really care. They looked at me before I was beaten up, and now for other reasons they looked at me again. I guess it will never stop. Some scars of sin are like that. They never heal, but they can be used for God's glory.

Thanks to Mr. Anderson and his intervention on my job, I didn't come into contact with many people other than my family, friends, and other employees at the agency. At church they grew accustomed to my face and gradually, over the course of a year or more, I began to accept the way I looked. I couldn't do much about it anyway. Aaron did a good job with false teeth, and a neat short trimmed beard covered most of the scars, while fashionable tinted glasses hid the half closed eye for the most part. But sometimes because of the scarred face and that partly closed eye I often referred to myself as the ugly pirate.

This began to bother Gwen, and in her gentle wife-like way she asked me to stop putting myself down so much. "I didn't marry an ugly pirate," she'd say. "I married the Hunter Lowe I knew and loved in high school — and love now."

Learning to trust Gwen's judgment and wisdom, I told her one day, "Okay, it's a permanent wink."

On the afternoon of July thirtieth I drove Gwen, now very pregnant with our twins, to Ravenswood for the tenth year reunion of our high school class. Because August first, and the revelation about Skeeter was only two days away, I was a nervous wreck. The promotional TV releases were already made, and being kept under the watchful hand of Mr. Anderson. I did have his permission though, to sneak the secret to the class.

Seymour Wilts, and another friend of his, met us at the school and we enjoyed a few minutes of a mini reunion of our own. I introduced Seymour to as many as I could, but he and his traveling companion (aka parole officer because we were in a different state) said they would be just fine sitting at one of the tables until the time came for Seymour's part.

I had not seen most of these people since that graduation night ten years ago where as president of the class I read all their names, right here in the same room.

This was a dream come true for me, because there were days I thought I'd never see this place again. The gym smelled of the same heavy varnish, and the same victory banners of some of our championships still hung high on the walls.

The friends had all heard parts of my story and knew what to expect, so the introductions and hugs were wonderful. But deep down I felt a current of unrest. Good people just don't warm up very quickly to one who has been in prison, even though we were once friends. Only Bruce, in his ever not-so-gentle manner still called me the pirate. I don't think I'll ever stop loving him for his open frankness.

In a rare, quiet moment in that crowd, Aaron asked me how I honestly felt about my changed face. I told him, "Sometimes it bothers me, of course, but those of us with handicaps or 'interrupted lives,' must come to a point where we accept it as a new normal if we are to overcome the issue. The important change is in my heart. What God has done for me inside is far more important and exciting than my outer looks. I really do feel that, and I'm even happier now with my whole life in order."

Gwen and I milled around the crowd, and I'm sure we met just about everyone who was there that night. Mr. Hall, now retired, was our honored guest for the evening. He was the teacher who told me, as a sophomore, what gift I had in my looks. He was also the one who introduced me to Mr. Anderson who did so much for me before and after my time in prison.

Because of the accident and all the misery it caused,

and my dislike for anything to do with alcohol, Gwen and I held on to our Diet 7Up cans lest anyone got the idea we would have anything more to do with beer. I had no intention of turning this beer issue into a raging demonstration, but I wanted to make my statement. Gwen, in her pregnant condition and I were invited to sit at the head table with Mr. Hall and his wife Jan, as well as Bruce, the emcee for the evening, and his wife.

Dinner went well and was delicious. Even after a year or more out of prison, I was still enjoying real food: not a steady diet of turkey. Near the end of dinner an embarrassed caterer whispered something into Bruce's ear. And true to form, Bruce stood up and announced, "For some reason the desert has not gotten to the school yet. So being the guy in charge, I'll go on with the program. First of all, Hunter has a special friend he wants to introduce to you."

Chapter Forty

I walked to the microphone and said, "Before I give you the lowdown on my awesome life, I want you to hear a few words from a new friend of mine, Seymour Wilts."

As he walked – waddled – to the podium, the only thing the guests at their tables could see was the top of his bald head bobbing behind us. We all heard him say as he approached, "I hear you guys snickering out there. I'll get you for that."

When he finally got to the podium all we could see was his hands on it. At that point even his hands disappeared when he bent over and dragged out a purple plastic milk crate from under the table and stood on it. More laughter, only broken up by his remark, "Hey, it's either this or you won't know who's talking." Looking around, he said, "Ya know, I'm just three inches higher than half of Hunter. This milk crate helps me see the world kind of like he does."

After pausing while we all laughed, he raised his hand to silence us. Then he continued. "About two and a half years ago I met Hunter when we both lived in the same gated community in another state. We were on the same baseball team. Can you believe that? Me on a baseball team? They used me for second base, − not the position − the base." With his very round facial expressions and squeaky voice, he went on. "Now the state called that a correctional institution. Yeah right, I can tell you, very little correction really went on there."

The crowd opened up quickly to him and a wave of comfort and appreciation swept over the crowd. He went on with a short pile of funny stories from his comedy routine, and then he finished with, "You've just heard the clean side of my history. When I was dragged into Putnam Prison my disgusting mouth knew no borders. I mean it. I could make sailors and prison guards blush. I spent so many years developing my speaking ability, I could peal paint off steel bars, and wallpaper off walls three blocks away. I could break light bulbs thirty feet away with my highly honed vocabulary that was never identified from any known language or dialect. I'm telling you, good people, calling me a potty mouth would be an honor."

From the back of the room and the table with a high pile of dead beer cans, a voice yelled, "What broke you from swearing like that?"

"What?" the little guy asked with eyes in the form of a question.

The question was repeated, "How come you don't swear like that anymore? I'd like to hear some of it."

"Oh no you wouldn't. I could be arrested for public indecency or child abuse right here and now. Besides, there are ladies here − some gentlemen too."

"Come on, tell us, what cleaned you up?" a few others said. "Yeah, yeah, what was it like?"

"We ever met before?"

In a chorus, "No."

"Is this a setup question?"

Again, a ringing, "No."

"Well look out, but remember you asked for it. Hold onto your chairs for this. Thanks to your friend Hunter here, and a great guy named, Tyrone Williams, some real correction *did* take place in that dump on my vocabulary. One day the grace of God reached down and grabbed this filthy and debauched heart of mine, and on the way out cleaned up my voice better than the best drain cleaner you've ever known. Wham, bang, bam! That's all there was to it."

The silence was deafening.

Seymour went on, "This little guy is here to tell ya, call it what you want, cover it up with what you will, try any other method, use any toy, or figure any way around it, but that's the way it happened. I know some of you are saying or thinking, 'I don't believe all that Jesus religious stuff.' A few years ago I swore to that too.

"I'll leave you with what I heard from a guy who knew he was going to die in prison and be buried in a pine box far out in a corner of the prison yard when I said the same thing to him. 'Someday, Seymour, someday, you *will* believe this Jesus stuff. You'll face Jesus as your savior or as your judge.' Young people here in the gym, someday ... someday, you will too."

He closed with, "Thanks for your attention and

appreciation, but your old friend Hunter has something to tell you that will really crack these walls." Amid the applause, he suddenly disappeared from sight as he pushed the purple milk crate back under the table and the bald head bobbed its way back to his chair.

Chapter Forty-One

I stood at the microphone for a few seconds savoring the wonderful atmosphere Seymour had left them with, and wondered if the next secret was going to have any impact. They knew I did voiceovers, but this was going to come as a big surprise. I said, in a whisper, "Lean forward because I have a national secret to tell you."

I saw them unconsciously literally lean towards me. I cleared my throat and in Skeeter's voice repeated one of the lines that had the entire nation guessing. "Here I put my whole life in peril to mess up dat car, and I find out dat dey got *Your State Insurance* — what's da use?"

For two or three seconds, an eternity — stunned silence. *What, no reaction" They're just looking at each other like fish on a string.* Then, like a bomb going off, the whole place went up for grabs with wild applause, cheering, yelling, whistling, paper cups and plates flying in the air with confetti and napkins. From all around the gym I could hear people yelling.

"Skeeter!"

"It's Hunter."

"No way."

"I can't believe it."

"We're the first in the whole country to know who Skeeter is. It's Lowe."

"It's you."

"We love ya, Hunt."

"Lowe is Skeeter."

"Ravenswood's on the map."

"No kidding."

People pounded each other on the back, banged their hands on the tables and stormed us at the head table. The room was full of crazies. Bulky Aaron leaped over the head table and in midair, before he landed squarely on a used salad plate, gave me a high five. I looked at Mr. Hall and saw tears in his laughter as he was hugging his wife. Seymour jumped back onto his milk crate and joined the riot, twisting his napkin around his head. Our old high school class was itself again, and I was so glad to be a part of it.

When the explosion was over and the earthquake died down, I reminded them gently, "Now that you all know what the whole country wants to know, you've got to promise not to tell anyone for two days."

Okay Lowe, take a deep breath. Time to speak about the real stuff here.

"Thank you all so very much for inviting me here tonight. Also thanks for letting my good friend Seymour open this gig with his shiny new vocal chords." A sudden cheering applause erupted. "I also want to say thanks to so many of you for your thoughts and concerns for me over the past few years. Sometimes I wondered if others cared, but deep down I always had the feeling that friends were thinking of me, praying for me, and wishing me well. Turning to Gwen, I said, "And thanks especially to this great person next to me for her unwavering love and support in what was a terribly embarrassing few years."

As if on command, the whole class stood at once in a resounding standing ovation for her. Resting my hand on her shoulder, I continued, "Thank you, Gwen. I love you." Looking back to the crowd, "Thank you to the reunion committee for the invitation to speak and tell you my story. It might be different than what you're expecting.

"A lot of people here in Ravenswood and in Capital City have asked me, 'How did you make it through all that misery we've heard you've been through?' Well, dear friends, like Seymour said, 'Hang on to your chairs. I don't know how you make it through the jungles of your lives, but I made the journey and came out a better man because of Jesus." Jabbing a finger at the crowd a few times, "Yep, because of Jesus."

I could see some jaws drop, and eyes open wide, and even saw some frowns, but I had stepped up to the plate and it was time to take my swing. "I know you didn't come here tonight for a sermon, but I can't help giving credit to whom credit is due. It *is* my story.

"You all know me from my early life and high school years. To many of you who might have suffered from my arrogant and selfish ways in those days — I'm sorry. You know, we're all considered a lump of clay, but some of us have to get punched, beat up, spun around, soaked, stretched, twisted, and molded more than others, then put through the fire before we wise up.

"After graduation I was successful in the world of modeling, traveled all over the world strutting my stuff, smiling and looking like a dork standing in front of flashing lights and clicking cameras. Wherever I went, people waved and hollered and tried to get close and touch Hunter Lowe. What a pitiful waste.

"Then one night, because of a few lousy beers, the bright lights, traveling, and clicking cameras stopped as fast as pulling a plug. Two months later it got even worse as some wild man tore off my mask and put me into this permanent wink. I think life in a prison cell is where they got the expression, 'the pits.' I can't begin to tell you fine people how it is to live in a human septic tank."

Standing there in clean, tailored clothes, Gwen at my side, old friends all around, and in the high school of many memories, I suddenly lost my voice in choking emotions. In a higher pitched voice, quivering chest, eyes tightly shut, and teeth tightly clenched, I was able to get out, "I just will not take you there, friends.

"In the dark days of my life, in the cages of that zoo, there were a few, *very* few strokes of compassion. One older African American gentleman, and I do mean gentleman, named Tyrone Williams showed me, through his life and attitude that there was hope in that awful place. Reverend Crowley, a small town preacher came to the prison every other Sunday and brought sunshine into that dungeon wherever he stepped. Gabe Jackson, who most of you know from the NFL, came to the prison one day and of all things, sang songs with a guitar. He told us what a man Jesus really was.

"You don't know," I gulped and pinched my lips for a few seconds with my fist. I started again. "You don't know who Ben Marshall is, but one day he came to the prison with a friend of mine. I honestly thought he would finish the beating that the wild man started on me. You see, Ben Marshall is the husband of the woman I killed in that car crash in Capital City." I choked a bit again and then with God's help, went on. "Where I expected anger and hate, he showed me love and grace. Where I expected resentment, he offered forgiveness.

"Forgiveness, friends — forgiveness. Yes, Ben Marshall and his two kids offered me forgiveness. When I asked why, he simply told me that he knew the forgiveness Jesus offered him for his sins, and he knew how miserable I felt because of the accident. He said he wanted me to know the release that forgiveness offers." Holding my quivering hands out to the crowd, palms up, I said as I choked, "How does a guy handle that?"

Even though I was speaking to a bunch of my old goofy high school friends, I couldn't control the flowing of tears. So I grabbed a napkin, took my glasses off, and pressed it to my eyes. "I'm not ashamed of these tears. I hope I'll never be. I'm just so overwhelmed at the way God worked in my life because He cares and loves me so much.

"Let me go on before I chicken out and quit. In that prison cell, empty time had a way of wringing out all kinds of memories from my past and bringing them into focus. As I lay on my bunk, the minutes turned to hours, days, weeks, months, and years of depression and fear. In those same years you were running around free and advancing in your lives. I was reduced to looking at the little pours in concrete blocks and smooth mortar joints. Pieces of the puzzle came together through some very old memories of Sunday school. Believe it or not, the only conclusion I came to was that Jesus must have cared a lot for me, even after the stupid and ignorant stuff I'd done. The Bible tells me in many places that God has a plan for my life, and Jesus is the key to that plan."

While speaking from the head table at Ravenswood High I continued to choke up from time to time, and had a hard time going on.

Pregnant as she was, Gwen stood up and held my hand.

"Dear friends at Ravenswood High." I continued, "This Jesus stuff we all thought was foolishness when we were kids, is for real. Because He cared, in His own way, Jesus took this good-looking but arrogant smart aleck and put him through the grinder that made him the complete and happy man you now see. Jesus is truly the Light of the World we all need in these dark jungles we live in."

I noticed most of the friends in the audience were hanging onto every word I said, and I shot a quick prayer of thanks to God. I also noticed at that far table in the rear, a group of old R.H.S. football heroes snickering and depleting their supply of beer. Suddenly an instant thought ran through my mind. *What's beer doing in a high school gym?* Just as fast the accompanying thought: *What do those guys care about rules? Others just looked the other way that night.* They had stacked the dead cans up in the traditional pyramid so high I lost sight of the old quarterback, Phil Kish. *Don't let that stop you, Lowe, go on.*

"The most powerful thing I learned is that we all need to be saved from our sins. Yeah, we got 'em. Good guy, bad guy, good girl, bad girl. God loved this world so much He provided the sacrifice for our sins. He did all the work. He paid the price for our redemption. No other god, guru, or cult leader died to give their group forgiveness — but out of His grace, Christ did. Those other leaders want their followers to do all the sacrificing. We all have come up short of finding our own way to God, and none of us can get to Him without Jesus. He can be yours if you invite Him into your life. I'm glad to tell you tonight that just a month ago, Jesus saved the wild man called Charlie Sullivan who tore off my face and closed this eye. In conclusion tonight, let me say, if Jesus can save Charlie Sullivan and me, He can save you too."

I paused a short minute than said, "Thank you. Thank you friends, from the bottom of my heart. I remember this place and all of you with great affection."

The room was silent as Gwen and I sat down. Even the waiters at the doors, with the dessert that had now arrived, stood like the Sphinx. As I looked at that petrified crowd, I bit my lip. *Oh, Lord, what have I done? Did I let you down?*

Bruce was the first to recover, of course. "Hunter,

215

that will be hard to follow, but I see the dessert is here, so let's enjoy it."

Chapter Forty-Two

After the dessert, the evening was alive with thanks and best wishes. I even had the opportunity to encourage many old friends to follow up on what I said by searching out a church that taught Jesus. While milling around at the end of the evening in the gym, many came to thank me for telling my story. Others just wanted to say, "Hi," and told me it was good to have that Skeeter mystery over. Sharon Cox had an interesting statement. "I knew that voice sounded familiar. It was Squeak the village idiot that you played in the school play, wasn't it?"

Others said they'd been following the events of my life thanks to Aaron and Bruce. Ravenswood's famous and good-looking quarterback of ten years ago, Phil Kish, galloped up to me caressing his beer can. "Ya know, Lowe, I never did beeelieve in all that religgusfious stluff, and I still don't. Itz okay for others, I guezz. Did yhou try to convert me tonight?" Just the whiff of beer off his breath brought vivid memories back to me after all those years of that night in *Tommy's Tap* so many years ago.

"No, Phil, I can't convert anyone. Only the Holy Spirit can do that."

"Huh?" Phil's mouth dropped open like a broken mouse trap, and his his eyes rolled back in his head. "Zee, there you go again, Lowe."

"Phil, I'm sorry you don't believe in all this religious stuff, as you call it. Christ changed my life and now it all makes sense. What you do with Christ is up to you. But remember, you've been told and invited. Besides, the reunion committee just asked me to tell my story and I did it the only way I know how."

It looked like life had ridden Phil pretty hard. What was once a bright and talented athlete that took R.H.S. to the state finals just ten years ago was now quite portly, balding, and had gone through two divorces. He was being supported by his eighth or ninth beer of the evening and wasn't catching a thing I said.

"That Skeeter gig yhou do for that insurance company — good idea. Geth rich on that?"

"Your State has been good to us, but I wouldn't call it rich."

"Whone more thing, Lowe. I ztill drink like I done in high school, only lotz more now, zee? I'll say it again tonight — one hor two beers never hurt nobody."

I put my hands on his shoulders, bore down with just enough pressure to bend his back a little, looked squarely into his droopy and glassy eyes, and said quietly, "Phil, don't you see what three beers did to me a few years ago?" I took off my glasses and continued with, "Take a good long look at this face and tell me that again. Look Ben Marshall in the face and tell him and his kids what you just told me. You can't convince this face that a few beers are nothing. How has drinking enhanced your life?"

He stared at me as if I'd hit him with a brick. He looked down at his can of beer, back at me, then turned and walked away saying, "I don't give thiz up for nothing."

When Gwen and I left the school that night, we walked the four blocks to my folk's home, hand in hand through the streets of Ravenswood like we used to do in another world. As we walked under the familiar streetlights on Elm Place, we restated the list of the good reasons that came from my being in prison that she wrote in the Bible she sent me.

After we arrived home we joined Gwen's folks and mine on our back porch, and talked about the dinner, and the coming twins. Not only would they have a Christian mom, they would have a Christian dad!

When we went to bed, Gwen and I spent the night in my old bedroom.

On the way back to Capital City the next day, I told Gwen, "I really should go back to the prison and see Tyrone, and find out how Charlie Sullivan is doing as a new believer. I don't think I've done enough for them with my few letters. I don't want them to think I've forgotten them."

A week later reverend Johnson called and asked if we could meet for lunch. The time was set, and I met him at a restaurant where he introduced me to an older gentleman.

"Hunter, I'd like you to meet a retired Pentecostal

pastor friend of mine from a church at the far side of the city, Reverend Charles Sullivan Senior."

"Charlie's dad?" I asked.

"I would be the one, son."

As we sat at the table and worked over our BLTs I could only look at the old man and admire him as he told me of his life. I looked into a very old set of eyes that had searched scriptures and preached for generations. I saw eyes that had shed many tears for a wild and rebellious son.

From within a wrinkled face I saw a twinkle in his eyes when he said, "I understand, young man, you were the one who took my boy to the feet of Jesus one day."

"Reverend Sullivan, it was the thrill of my life."

"There is more to the story." He handed me a much-folded piece of paper. "I'd like you to read this letter I received from Charlie three weeks ago.

"To Papa, you no I cant rite long leters but I gotta say I reelly sorry for what I done 2 you and Ma. The imbarasmnt musta been reel bad. You and Ma tried awful hard to teach me rite but I guess I was so dum. My friend Tyrone says you musta prayed a lot for me cuz now I'm Christian. I no I'm in jail for lots more years but I feel so good in my heart. Someday I hope you see that Hunter Lowe. I beet him up awful bad when he got here. Now he forgvs me. I glad 2 here you are coming here in 2 weeks for visit. I'll be reelly happy 2 see you. From Chuckie."

I handed the worn letter back to him. "Reverend Sullivan, please let me know when you're going to see Charlie. I'd love to go with you."

Stopping me with a hand on my arm, he continued, "Two weeks ago there was another bad fight at the prison. The Department of Corrections kept it out of the media, but as two new inmates were beating up a guard, Charlie tried to stop the fight. The new inmates killed my Charlie. I came so close to seeing him again."

I reached over the table and took this old and trembling man by the hands. "Pastor Sullivan, I'm so very sorry Charlie died that way. His life knew so much pain. I'm sorry."

"Don't be sorry, son," the old pastor said, with a sudden sparkle in his tear-filled eyes, "I'll see him again someday. Remember, there's *Victory in Jesus!*"

Made in the USA
Columbia, SC
27 July 2019